The Brewster Boys

and the

Eve of Infamy

STEPHEN DITTMER

Mom and Dad: Thanks for your love, support and encouragement in my every endeavor.

CHAPTER ONE

"Shut the door!"

"What? Why?"

"Just do it. Do it!"

I watch as Pete pulls himself up and then off of the final rung of the rope ladder, slamming the main door to the treehouse. He does so with an extra oomph, presumably to show his contempt and bewilderment. With that slam we're lucky the whole treehouse doesn't crash to the ground.

Pete is my cousin, but more like a little brother. Even though he's a year younger than I and about two inches shorter, people always think we are twins. I don't know. I guess we do have the same last name of "Brewster."

We are cousins. His dad and my dad are

4

brothers. We are both tall and skinny with dark brown hair, so, I guess I can understand why some people would be under that impression. Pete has braces though; luckily I got mine removed this past January. I just finished my freshmen year of high school. Pete starts his in the fall.

I guess we are your average teenagers. We love sleeping, eating, hanging out, the latest electronics, music, movies, sports and reading. Ok, well, I guess I enjoy reading more than the average teen. You know the sort. We are not the popular types nor are we the lowest rank on the food chain that is, "high school." We are at a safe median, exactly where we want to be. But unlike the majority of kids our age, most of our summer days are spent in our treehouse.

"What's the deal, Jon?" asks Pete.

"Look out door three," I whisper.

Every entrance to our treehouse has a number assigned to it. I don't know why. It's just something we created as kids, like a special privileged code if we ever had visitors. But we're much older now and don't rely on our childish system anymore. Now, the numbers simply serve as a designation to let us know which window or door we are talking about. As we grew, lots of things changed, but the serenity and independence of the treehouse never left us. It is worn down and unkempt but we still use it to escape the daily doldrums of our everyday existence.

We built the treehouse one fall while in

elementary school. Ok. So, *we* didn't build it, our dads did: my dad and Uncle Rob. Pete and I just kind of watched and handed our fathers the requested screwdriver, wrench or hammer. And, when we were lucky, we would occasionally get to push the button on the power tools. It's funny those old power tools are now mine. Dad upgraded his years ago.

The treehouse itself is typical: rectangular in shape, rope ladder, has lots of windows and is made of squeaky wooden planks. It sits atop an old oak tree, the biggest one in my backyard. The tree is so old and tall that the first branches available to build on were as high as the second story of my house. Needless to say, it is pretty high up for a treehouse. When we were younger, our dads took turns supervising, or babysitting us, however you want to put it.

Pete nears door three, which is really a window with a hanging-type door made out of your basic plywood. He slowly pushes the door up and away from the rest of the treehouse and peers outside. The view is slightly obscured due to the lush green leaves on the main supporting branch.

"What am I looking for, exactly?" asks Pete.

"Shhh! Not so loud! See anything unusual?" I ask.

"No . . . um . . . wait! Wait. Yeah! Dude! The Wilton's swimming pool is finally finished! Pete, this summer is gonna be epic, man! We gotta g . . . "

"No!" I exclaim. "Why in the world would I

6

be whispering about a swimming pool?" Pete, looking confused, shrugs his shoulders.

I have to admit, it is pretty amazing that the pool is finally finished. Mr. Wilton, my neighbor, has been trying to finish it for the past two years. Here it is, the first week of July, two years later and it's finally done. Maybe this is our lucky summer. But still, that wasn't what I meant.

I slowly creep over towards Pete who is still staring out door three, mesmerized by the prospects of a summer full of sun and fun. I do my best to avoid knocking over our stacks of comic books and shove away a half eaten bag of stale BBQ potato chips. Approaching the door, I gaze up at Pete with his eyes wide open in amazement. He is definitely anticipating a fun summer of free swimming, right next door. I motion for him to scoot over and we exchange the task of holding the door open. I slowly scan the neighborhood and spot the pool, two houses over.

The treehouse gives us a great panoramic view of our street, Rickenbacker, as well as the whole neighborhood. This is especially true when so many of the houses are simple, one level ramblers. Not ours though. Our house is a quite large, two story colonial with a basement. Our treehouse sits in the backyard atop the 85 year old oak.

"See it?" Pete points over towards the Wilton's yard as I quickly scan past it.

"Yeah, finally," I mutter. He can tell by my

7

expression that I am, indeed, looking for something else.

As I continue to scan the area, Pete turns around and collapses onto one of our two giant bean bag chairs. He chooses the red one, the good one that is not being held together with silver duct tape. He picks up the stale bag of chips and takes a whiff. Surprisingly approving of their odor, he lays back and starts to eat.

"There!" I shout, but slowly realize it is no time for shouting. "Pete, come here!" I say in an insistent, yet softer voice. Turning around, I spot Pete smiling up at me while enjoying his chips and raising the bag high, offering me some. He can't hear me now because his earbuds are buzzing away at his eardrums with the latest one hit wonder, pop music sensation, "Suzie." I'd like to think I am more cultured than Pete. Sure, some pop songs are catchy and I can "get my dance on" while listening, but I prefer songs that have survived the test of time; songs from the 50's and 60's or even earlier are what I'm all about.

"Come here, man!" I speak up just a bit louder.

"What? What?" He responds. "Come on, Jon! I just wanna relax. I spent all morning mowing nine lawns! Nine! Game over, man. Game over. But hey, I did make some mad cash!" Pete reaches in his pocket and pulls out a freshly earned wad of fives, tens and twenties.

That's one thing he has right now that I don't
. . . a job.

"Peter, get over here right now!" I demand, while shooting him a stern and piercing look. He knows I am serious now. This is not only because of my expression or the tone of my voice, but because we never, ever call each other with the full lengths of our first names. It is always "Pete" or "Jon," never "Peter" or "Jonathan."

Pete reluctantly pushes himself off the bean bag chair and heads back towards door three. But just as he arrives, I simultaneously shut the cover and put my finger over my lips to make sure he knows to be quiet. I remove my finger and nod my head waiting for an acknowledgement. Pete nods back in agreement and leans in closer towards the window. We slowly push the door up. He wants to open it all the way but I only allow it to be slightly cracked. Pete leans over, peaks out the crack and waits.

"Now do you see, Pete?" A large white van with painted-over windows slowly creeps down the street. It comes to an abrupt stop right across from our treehouse. The driver and front passenger both exit. The rear doors of the van thrust open and three more men emerge, each hopping out of the back one at a time. Pete and I pull back the door a bit more to ensure we are not exposed as we continue to observe.

Pete starts humming the theme song from the *Men in Black* franchise. I let out a chuckle but quickly regain my focus. He is right, though. These guys look like they should be in a stretch limo and not a workmen's van. All of the men are sharply dressed with suits and ties. Their shiny shoes glisten in the summer sunlight. The five men scan the area while the driver barks orders.

"Who are they, Jon?"

"I dunno. But they were snoopin' around here yesterday too."

"What do they want?"

"Shhh! I dunno. I wish we could hear them."

Three of the men spread out in different directions. The driver remains with one leg resting upon the car. He casually smokes a cigarette. The only thing that distinguishes the driver from the rest of the bunch is his black, 1930's era, fedora, lined with a broad, white band. He is also sporting a fairly dark tan, too dark for this early in the summer. It looks legit too, unlike those orange guys from that reality show in New Jersey. A red Volvo passes by. The man with the fedora waves the car on as if he is directing traffic exiting a rock concert.

"Wish we had one of those miracle ear things like Grandpa Jacob, huh, Jon?"

"Yeah!" Just then it hits me. We *do* have one of those miracle ear things. Well, not exactly, but it does the same thing.

"Pete, remember those old matching spy kits Aunt Becky gave us like . . . six or seven Christmases ago?"

"Yeah and it had one of those....umm, yeah

10

one of those sound listening . . . uh . . . thingies!"
Pete recalls.

"Where are they?" I inquire.

"Who knows, man? Look at all this junk!"
Pete says as he shakes his head.

He's right. As I said before, we are your
average, typical teenage guys; this treehouse is a
mess. Mom would kill me. The only time she saw the
inside of the treehouse was when she climbed up the
ladder to bring everyone lemonade. That was a while
ago, during the house's construction. The walls
weren't even up at that point.

One of the joys of growing up, I guess, is
having to do things on your own. Cleaning the
treehouse or my room, however, is not one of those
joys. That four letter word, "responsibility" . . .
overrated. Those spy kits could be anywhere. Even if
we do find them, I can't remember if they even
worked.

Pete crosses to the other side of the treehouse
and begins to dig through a random pile of junk,
while I continue to keep a sharp eye on our
questionable new visitors. He shuffles through all of
our useless treasures: Japanese attack trading cards, a
smashed up ant farm that no longer has any
occupants, an old fad of colorfully shaped rubber
wrist bands and a werewolf Halloween mask, with
green gum stuck in its fur.

"Awwww yeaahhhh!" Pete turns around and
reveals a plastic briefcase containing a red horn that

resembles a small satellite dish. The case also includes a cheap pair of binoculars, some fake passports and a pair of broken handcuffs. He had found it, buried and tangled up with the wrist bands. Now we just need to see if the old thing still works. I hastily walk over and rudely grab it from his hands, revealing its name. "Ha, the old *Sherlock 3000*," I say.

"No, no," Pete butts in, "The *Shheerrrrllock 3000*," as he says in his comical movie announcer voice, one of his many impressions. He hands me the device and I hastily turn it on. We slowly creep over to door three and push it open, aiming the *Sherlock 3000* towards the men, who by this time are spread across the neighborhood. One is creeping around the Lee's house.

The Lees are a quiet, older Asian couple who are extremely friendly, but resented by most kids for giving out pennies on Halloween.

Two other men crossed through some backyards and are now walking down Bradenton Avenue, the street that runs parallel to Rickenbacker. The driver and one other guy, a stubby little man with a tiny goatee and greasy slicked back hair, are still at the van.

"Does it even have batteries?" asks Pete.

"I dunno. But no time to check." I switch it on and focus the device towards the two at the van, reasoning that if it does work, the more nearer to the target, the better. For a moment, I feel like Pete and I are kids again, on another misadventure in our treehouse. But no, this could be serious. Something is up and we both know it.

"Crzzkkkkkkkk, crzzkk, crzzzzkkkkkk." The old toy crackles with static. The *Sherlock* had seen better days, but at least we know it has batteries. Pete reaches in between my arms and starts messing with the dials. Just as I am about to pull it away from him, the static is replaced with audible English.

"Because if we don't, Leo, somebody else will," demanded the man with the old school hat and a thick Long Island accent.

"Ok, ok. I understand. I understand," Leo says while looking down and kicking the van's tire.

"Now get out there and go find the damned thing!"

"Alright, boss. But lemme warn ya, the boys are concerned."

Just then a late model, green Jaguar with deep tinted windows pulls up alongside the van and comes to a stop.

"Great. Just what we need. It's her. I got betta things to worry about now." says the man with the hat.

"Yeah, well, I'll get lookin'," finishes Leo as he jogs across the street and signals the guy in the Lee's yard.

The Jaguar's passenger door opens and out steps a tall blonde with a very striking red dress and matching hat. And I thought the van full of suited

13

men was out of the ordinary. What is it with these people and fancy hats? She looks like she should be in Hollywood or Beverly Hills or someplace like that. Her white stilettos seem to make her about four inches taller, putting her eye to eye with the driver of the van. She is indescribably attractive: classy and sort of upscale. Somewhat of a cross between Marylyn Monroe and . . . and . . . well, Marylyn Monroe. Everything but the sultry voice that is, and I mean everything.

"*Crzzzzkkkkk, Crzzzzk...*" crackles the toy.

"Well, did you find it?" the lady asks while removing her, no doubt, designer sunglasses.

"Not yet, but were on it. I got my best guys out there right now," says the driver.

"Your best guys, ay? Yeah, I saw one of your 'best guys' take a little rollie-pollie jog across the street. You better not let me down Jackson, 'cuz if you mess this thing up . . . I swear, if I had my pick again I . . ."

"Yeah, yeah, I heard it all before." He interrupts. "There is one thing I should tell ya. We think we know what the problem is. There is a short in the thermal switch. So every time . . ." *Beeeeummmmmpppp.*

That's it. The batteries are dead. The tall boss man, Jackson, as he was called, turns from the women and pulls a walkie talkie out of the van's driver's side door compartment. He brings it to his mouth and speaks into it. At that moment, all of the

14

other men start returning to the van. Clearly he was speaking to them through the walkie. Before the men make it back to the van, the lady in red hops in the Jag and speeds off.

The men return and Jackson addresses the stubby man, Leo, I think he was called. The others climb into the back of the van. Leo, once again, shrugs his shoulders. Jackson raises his hand as if he is going to slap him but he restrains himself at the last minute. Jackson takes one more passing glance around the adjacent yards and reclaims his role as driver, taking off in the opposite direction of the lady in red.

"Wow! What do you think that was all about, Jon? Huh?"

"I dunno, man . . . they are obviously looking for something."

"Yeah," Pete interrupts, "something with a thermal switch! Could it be a bomb or something? I mean, thermal, that's like, nuclear right? Just like from that movie, *Attack of the Nuclear Zombies* or the sequel, *Revenge of the Nuclear Zombies*! Or is it like . . . like, some sort of uranium or plutonium radiation power source or something? Huh? Whatcha think, Jon?"

Pete is losing it.

I don't say a word. Pete takes a diving leap back onto the bean bag chair. I sit and stare out door three, wondering, worrying, fearing and at the same time hoping, that maybe this event could be as exciting as it seems.

Why do we constantly look for something more, for a sort of adventure? Is it just Pete and I or is it everyone? Pete has the same attitude that every kid our age has: nothing to do in our town, it's so boring here, nothing exciting here ever happens. Dad always says, "It's always greener on the other side of the street," meaning that wherever you are, whatever you have, whatever you are doing, you feel like someone always has it better than you. I can understand that. It's funny, all year long we pray for summer vacation and once it starts, a week later, we are bored and ready to go back to class.

Now it's getting late. Ok, it's not really late. It's only around 9:20 p.m. But we always like to get down from the oak before it gets pitch black outside. We have been accustomed to doing so ever since Pete took a major spill a few years back. He ended up with a broken arm, elbow and pinky finger. That was not a fun time for either of us. I had to copy notes for him in all of our shared classes. After that, I think I needed the cast and sling more than he did! Mom blamed it on the darkness, so ever since then, we promised her we would come down before dusk. The only exception to that rule is when we stay up here for the entire night.

"Ok, Jonny boy, it's closing time," Pete says as he slaps me on the back imitating an old west gold prospector, one of his favorites.

"You read my mind Petey-Pete, Pete old

16

boy," I say, doing my best to compliment his impression. "I guess it's about that time."

That's one thing I love about summer. Here it is pushing nine thirty and the sun is just now setting. If this was winter, the sun would have set hours ago. I always wonder about that. I mean, if time and calendars and clocks and days are all human creations, why can't we change it to have sunset at 9:30 every night?

"Let me know if you see those guys anymore, Jon," Pete says as he exits the oak. "Yeah, man. Sure will." The whole event was quite curious. What was it all about anyways?

CHAPTER TWO

My cell phone's alarm clock rings 11:00 a.m. This is after I hit the snooze for the fourth time in a row. Another reason as to why I love summer is sleeping in. And I needed it this morning. It took me forever to fall asleep last night. I kept wondering about those men, that elegant, yet sinister lady and whatever it was they were so worried about finding. "Just ten more minutes," I mumble as I close my eyes again.

"Jonathan," my mom calls out from downstairs, "Wake up, Sleepy! Come on, the pooch needs to go out. Take her for a walk." I lift my leg off the bed and bang the floor just a bit to acknowledge that the message was received. I hear my pup, our little Miniature Dachshund, Feebie, sniffing under my bedroom door, occasionally pawing at it. I guess I gotta get up.

After going through my normal routine of waking up: showering, getting dressed and feeding the beta fish in the aquarium on my dresser, I head downstairs to the kitchen. "Thanks, Mom," I shout,

18

taking a bite out of a cherry danish she left on the counter for me.

"You're welcome and don't forget to walk Feebie!" she calls from the laundry room.

"I am right now, Mom. Come on, Feebz!"

Attaching the pink harness to Feebie, I open the front door and head outside. The aroma of wild honeysuckle permeates the air. I take our usual path crossing the street, walking past the Lee's and the Wilton's, past the bank of community mail boxes and continue down the road. I always stop at the playground and let Feebie sniff around. She never has a problem finding a new smell to investigate, hidden deep in the blanket of dried out mulch.

Feebz goes up to every swing sets' support pole, both the red and yellow slides and her favorite, the blue springy rocking horse. The playground sits in front of a manmade community lake, outlined by a scattering of several huge boulders. On the other side of the lake, I spot Pete mowing one of the biggest lawns in the neighborhood. It belongs to an historic plantation house.

The house lies on the older side of the neighborhood and dates back to the turn of the century or maybe even older. Pete is only lucky enough to mow its lawn every few weeks. He has it easy though. When I mowed lawns a few years back, I had three other guys competing against me to mow that lawn. Pete only has one competitor, and a lazy one at that. So, needless to say, Pete has been raking in the dough this summer. This was already his third time mowing the old plantation house lawn due to a few nights of heavy summertime downpours. He would be there for quite a while.

"Whatcha doing?" says a familiar voice.

"Oh. Hey, Abby."

Abby Wellington, the kid sister I never had . . . and never wanted. Well, I guess I am being a bit too hard on her. It's just that she can be a tad annoying, to say the least. She always does her best to tag along when she's not wanted and pops up at the least expected and worse moments. I guess you could say she is kind of like that pimple on the first day of school or photo day. Ok, well, she is not that bad.

She is Pete's age and about an inch taller than he. She has this subdued orange hair put up in these old-school, childish pigtails. Even though I kind of pick on her myself, I stick up for her all the time. If anyone even thinks of calling her a "ginger" or anything to that effect, they have to answer to me. She also wears these heavy, dark-framed glasses and has braces. She used to have a crush on me. And Pete used to have a crush on her. But that's in the past . . . I hope. She has been spending more and more time with me and Pete ever since her parents started their procedures for divorce. I'm so glad my folks are together. That must suck.

"Not much, just walking Feebz on this glorious summer morning. How 'bout you, Abb?"

"Nooooothing. Just hanging out on the porch swing and thought I would tell you that Astro Comics just got there shipment in, a day early!"

"Shut up! How do you know?" I ask as I encourage Feebie to move on after being distracted by a Monarch butterfly, crossing our path.

Abby knows comics. She also knows how much Pete and I love to be at the comic shop when the new deliveries come in, especially in summer when we have a bit of extra money to spend: Pete from lawns, and I from walking dogs. It has been slow for me so far though. I guess not many people are going out of town with the inflation of gas prices and all.

"I know because my dad called my mom from work. He was late because the delivery truck blocked his parking space at his office next door. Apparently they have a new delivery man or something."

"And the new guy delivers early?" I ask. "Aw, man, why didn't you text me, Abby?"

"Haters gonna hate!" she says, while making a duck face.

She wasn't serious, of course. It was her usual sarcasm. Nobody would take her seriously if she really used slang like that, especially the way she looked. I couldn't pull it off either. I dunno. If you can say it without being laughed at, then, well, go for it. She preferred the sarcastic approach and never expected anyone to take her seriously, even when she

21

used it in proper context.

"We gotta get over there, Abby," I insist.

"Well, uh . . . I already got my weeklies, so you and Pete are on your own. Hey there's Sara! Hey Sara! See ya, Jon," she shouts as she runs across the street. Nice change of subject. I don't even see Sara anywhere. She knows I am jealous that she got her weekly editions before Pete and I did.

Finishing up our walk, with Feebie's tongue hanging out of one side of her mouth, I open the back gate and chase her inside the house. She heads straight to her bowl and begins to slurp up the water.

"Up the oak, Mom," I yell over the locomotive-like sound of our antique vacuum. Dad tried to buy Mom a new one last Christmas but she refuses to use it. It sits, to this day, unopened, in the garage next to Dad's unopened weed eater. They were made for each other.

She always says, "If it ain't Baroque, then don't fix it," one of her favorite play on words, seeing that she always listens to Bach when she vacuums.

Upon entering the treehouse, I stop and look around. It hits me. I don't want to spend all summer in this elevated shanty. But if I was going to, it was time to do some serious cleaning of my own. Doors three through five are already open, letting in the sun as well as the fresh air. I open the top hatch to let even more sunlight pierce through the dank structure. Pete and I installed the hatch ourselves last summer. It seemed like a good idea at the time, but when it rains, boy do we regret it. We should have listened to Dad and used some sort of rubber or putty sealant.

"Time to start cleaning," I declare as I survey the disaster zone. But where to begin: organize the comics, throw away the trash, knock down that wasp nest that gets bigger and bigger each day?

"Oh, wow," I mutter in a less than enthusiastic tone. In the corner, underneath a fallen poster of an F-16 Thunderbird, lies my history book. Now, spotting a history book would normally not put me in a bad mood. I love history. I mean, love it! That is probably the biggest difference between Pete and I. He could care less. But if I could spend time in every decade in every century there ever was, I would be the happiest guy around. The book, however, reminded me of my homework. Knowing that I had to complete a summer assignment in any class, for that matter, dampened my cheery demeanor.

Just then, out of the corner of my eye, I notice the same green Jaguar coming down the street. It parks a few houses up from mine. Out steps the "lady in red." Although this time, she is in a blue business suit. I grab the companion pair of binoculars from the recently recovered spy kit and raise them to my eyes. All I know is, if I were female, I would never wear one of those things. They look worse than the suits I have to wear for my band recital. Those things are stuffy enough.

She walks to the rear of the car, opens the trunk and shuffles through, what appears to be, a few

23

different cardboard and magnetic signs. I can't make them all out but one reads, "Engine Detailing." In her getup, she definitely does not look like the car detailing sort. She drops another one to the ground that reads, "Fresh and Clean Maid Service." I don't know about you, but I have never seen a maid fortunate enough to be cruising around in a car of that caliber. She decides on a blue and red sign and slaps it to the side of her car. It reads "Samantha Realty, Serving Your Community Since '97."
Just what is she up to?

CHAPTER THREE

I spy as she crosses the street and heads towards the Lee's house. She walks up over the curb and onto their front path. The whole time she nears the front door her head is facing down, turning back and forth and scanning the entire front lawn. Just before she reaches the door, Mr. Lee appears.

He approaches from the other side of the house while holding a rusty watering can. The Lees have this huge flower garden in their front yard, always full of butterflies and birds. They even have a little, granite Koi pond, that butts up against their house. I grab the trusty *Sherlock 3000*, freshly charged with batteries, borrowed from a radio controlled car, and listen in.

"Hello, can I help you?" Mr. Lee asks, catching her off guard.

"Oh, yes, hello. Sorry, I didn't see you there. I was just admiring your beautiful garden."

"Oh, thank you. I work very hard on it, everyday. I just got a new butterfly bush over there near the geraniums. You see it?

"I see that. How nice." she says, obviously

25

uninterested in Mr. Lee's green thumb. She extends her hand and says, "Let me introduce myself. I'm Samantha Leham of Samantha Realty. I am just in . . ."

"Oh no, we love our house, not selling anytime soon."

"And I don't blame you with such a great garden!"

"Let me go get my wife. She'd love to meet you too."

"Well, honestly, sir, I was just in the area because one of my agents lost something the other day while showing some first-time buyers around the neighborhood. I was wondering if you found anything in your yard or in the street or perhaps . . . maybe . . ."

"Hmmm no, no I don't think so. What is it? What's it look like?"

"*Crzkkkkkkkkkkkk Crzkkkkkkkk.*" The conversation is broken up with static.

"Yeah, so it's kind of small."

"Nope, sorry." says Mr. Lee.

"Ok, well here's my card in case . . . *Crrzzkkkkkkkk Beuuuuuuuumpp.*

Again! Geez! Maybe it's not the batteries after all. I guess I can't complain. We threw the spy kit in the corner and probably stepped on it a hundred times. The blue one is still missing.

After smacking the *Sherlock* with the palm of my hand, I give up and toss it to the ground. *Sherlock*

26

1800 is more like it. My attention is refocused on Samantha, or whatever her real name is. She crosses back over to our side of the street and approaches my house!

I move over to door one to get a less obstructed view of my house's front door. She continues with the same posture and walk as before, always scanning the ground to look for this, elusive, mysterious item. She makes it to my porch and rings the bell. A few moments later my mom answers and they start to converse. I definitely cannot hear them from this high up and my top secret spy tool is a bust. I assume she is asking the same questions she posed to Mr. Lee, without regards to the garden, of course. Ours is pretty standard.

They finish talking and my mom gives her usual cheery wave goodbye and shuts the door. The would-be real estate agent glances up at the treehouse as if she is looking right at me. I freeze as a chill crosses over my entire body. But she didn't see me . . . did she? Maybe I wasn't as stealthy as I had imagined. She continues her uncertain journey to the next house. What could a real estate agent lose that is so important? I have got to find out.

As I reach the last few rungs of the rope ladder, I jump off and run inside my house via the back door.

"Mom! Mom!" I check the laundry room. No luck. I head towards the kitchen. "Mom!"

"What, Jon? What?" Mom replies.

"Hey! Sorry, Mom. Who was that lady at the door? Who was she?"

"My, my, Jon. She was an attractive lady wasn't she?" she says with a sarcastic grin.

"No, Mom, for real. Who was she? What did she want?

"I dunno, Hun. Just some real estate agent who lost something."

"Yeah, I know. But what was it exactly? What was she looking for?"

"What do you mean . . . you know?" she asks as she goes to the cupboard and starts to pull out an old blue Tupperware-like storage container. "Jon, did you start that summer history project thing?" she asks, taking us off topic.

"Mom, summer barely started. I have plenty of time. Whaaaaat waaaaass sheee looooooking fooooor?"

"Oh, I dunno. Some . . . umm, what was it a . . . Why do you care anyways? Did you find it?"

"No, but just in case I do find it!"

I am getting frustrated now. I need to know what's so important. What were the lady and those other goons searching for?

"Come on, Mom!" I plead.

"Umm, I think it was a . . . gee what did she call it again? Ya know, one of those things."

"Really, Mom? Really? One of those . . . *things!!??*"

"Yeah, ya know, for measuring rooms in

houses and door frames and ceiling heights and things."

"Um . . . a tape measure?"

"Bingo!" She says with a finger on her nose and another finger pointing at me.

"So, she was knocking on our door to find a missing tape measure?" I asked incredulously.

"Yes. Strange, huh? Oh, she did say it was electronic or something, digital I think. I guess it was pretty expensive. Now go get started on your summer work or no new comics for this week."

"Ok, Mom, thanks. Back to the oak!"

Walking back to the tree, comic books and the summer assignment are the last things on my mind. I climb back up into the treehouse and am so focused on the events that have just conspired that I don't realize I have already made it to the top of the ladder. I push the door up and climb through the opening, heading towards the duct-taped blue bean bag chair. Just one day has passed and the good red one is already covered up with junk.

Falling on top of the cushy chair and hearing the crunch of the beans as they readjust to my weight, I look towards the ceiling and ask myself, "What does it mean?" My eyes start to follow the swaying model airplanes that are held up with some old, clear, fishing line. I focus on the one right above me, an *SR-71 Blackbird* that Pete and I built when we were younger. The crosswinds of the treehouse blow the model to the left and right over and over again. The

Blackbird begins to hypnotize me and puts me in a trance of my own deep thoughts.

"Yo, Jon! You up there?" It sounds like Abby again. Oh, well. So much for deep thoughts. "Jon? Helllllooooo?"

"Yeah, come on up," I reluctantly reply.

"What's up? Get those comics yet?" she says while making her way up the ladder.

Abby forcefully throws open the door and pops her head through, while lobbing a size five, white and green soccer ball at me. She waits there, with an expression of confusion on her face, propping her upper body on the floor while still standing on the rope ladder, half of her body in and half out. Normally, I would respond immediately and that's why she is so confused. It's not my soccer ball, so it's easy to tell that she wants to kick it around a bit. I don't know if I mentioned it, but she is a prime time tomboy, and a much better athlete than Pete and I combined. Abby loves a lot of things, like those comics. But soccer is her life.

I lay there as she awaits a reply.

"Ummm, are you mad at me for getting my weeklies before you, Jon? 'Cuz if you are that is just ridiculous. I mean . . ."

"No, no. Come on in," I say as I remove my eyes from their fixed position on the model airplane.

"Good. Thanks. For a minute there I thought you were reverting back to elementary school days with you and Petey's, 'no girls allowed' rule."

"Ha ha," I chuckle as she brings back pre-adolescent memories of thinking girls have cooties and you should stay as far as possible from them. Man, how things have changed.

"Well, you wanna play or what?" she asks as she pulls herself up and into the treehouse.

"No, not now."

"So you *are* mad at me."

"Naw, naw. I am just preoccupied with things, that's all, Abb."

"I see," she replies as she nods her head towards my unopened history book.

"Huh? No, not that," I explain.

"Well what then?" she asks with a hand on her hip.

Now I had something else on my mind: contemplating whether or not I should tell Abby what had happened up to this point. I let out a giant sigh and sit up from my relaxed position and face Abby. With hands clasped on my lap, I look up towards her and say, "Ok, Abb, only Pete and I know about this, but I guess I will clue you in, ok?"

"Ohhh, gossip, ay? Do tell!"

"No, no. I'm for real. This is serious stuff."

I begin to explain everything that happened, everything that I knew since yesterday: the white van and the men, the green Jag and the lady in red, the door to door visits, everything.

Abby silently takes it in, with her mouth gaping wide open, hanging on my every word as if

31

my speech is her oxygen or something. As I finish up and have nothing more to say, she looks at me with a smirk while shaking her head back and forth.

"Sounds like a good story, Jon, but ya can't fool me," she insists. "You tryin' to be a superhero or something? I never thought I would say this, but, maybe reading too many comic books *is* bad for you. You're starting to lose hold of reality, man. That chick is probably just a realtor and those guys probably just work for her."

"Whatever, Abby. Wow! I can't believe I even bothered wasting my time telling you. Come on. Let's go pass the ball. . . "

"Walllluuuu. Walllluuuu," interrupts a bird call. But not just any bird call. It was our bird call. Only the three of us, Pete, Abby and I, knew how to do it. We used it to find each other. Every year we signed up for the bird calling contest at the Berkley County Fair, a more rural county, adjacent to ours. We got the idea from watching a rerun of these teenage bird callers on the *David Letterman* show. The participants on that show honestly looked like idiots with their hands flapping wildly all over the place, shouting, cackling and cooing up their best bird mating and warning calls. Ours was more on par with the real thing. Our call started off as a joke so we could get on the show, but, we made it pretty far in the contest two years ago and really got into it. We even made it to the state finals.

"Pete must be done mowing the plantation

house," Abby declares.

"Yup," I agree, as we look outside.

"Walllluuuu. Wallluuuu," we reply. We do it so well that we blend in with the rest of the birds in the area. We sound exactly like a . . . well, it's actually a combination of several bird calls, but it sounds authentic nonetheless. Our main inspiration was an Appapane. It's this tropical red bird with a pretty unique call. It's indigenous to the Hawaiian Islands. Abby picked it out at random from an Audubon book she got for her birthday.

Sure enough, Pete comes climbing up the rope ladder. He is drenched in sweat and wearing his typical mowing-the-lawn outfit, consisting of a white tank top, blue overalls and shoes, so stained by grass you'd think he was just dipped in some sort of toxic goo. He also has his usual gallon jug of iced tea thrown about his shoulder, attached to an old back pack shoulder harness. He finishes his ascent into the treehouse, huffing and puffing like he just ran the Marine Marathon.

"Whew!" he says while wiping a mass of sweat from his brow as he closes the door behind him. "We need an elevator!

"Long day, huh, Pete," asks Abby.

"Hey, Abb, how ya been? What's new?" asks Pete, still out of breath from mowing lawns.

"Not much, just listening to you and Jon's *007* adventure," Abby jests, followed by a chuckle.

"Huh? Oh. Oh, yeah, ha ha." Pete, not really

getting the *James Bond* reference and preoccupied with his thirst, takes a seat on an overturned storage crate, removes his iced tea from his shoulder strap, unscrews the top and takes an enormous gulp.

"Well, I'm glad you guys spend your summer days lost in a world of make believe," Abby says, matter of factly, as she opens up an old issue of the comic, *Amazing Warlord Wizards*. It had fallen from the stack last night in Pete's search for the *Sherlock 3000.*

"Hey, you're one to talk, 'Queen of comics,'" I say with a huge grin.

Abby slams down the comic and says, "Um, you love comics too, smart guy."

"Yes, I do. It's my world of make believe, but *this* isn't make believe. For real, something is up. You'll see."

Pete takes another swig and asks, "What's up, guys?"

"I told Abb about those men and everything and what happened today."

"Why, what happened today?

"Oh, get this Pete. Our mysterious 'lady in red' showed up today . . .

"That hotty? What happened?"

"Ha, yeah, man. She slapped this fake real estate sign on her car and had a name badge and everything. She was going door to door looking for something. She even came to my house and asked my mom!"

34

"Looking for what?" Pete asked me in a more anxious manner than I asked my mom.

"Ok. Get this. She is supposedly looking for some dumb digital tape measure that her real estate agents, the five stooges from yesterday, had lost."

"Yeah, right. What kind of tape measure has a thermal switch on it, ha ha?"

"Exactly!" I turn and say as I turn back and stare at Abby. She again shakes her head in disbelief, while picking up a different issue of the same comic and begins thumbing through it.

"That's just it, Pete. That's the question of the year. It's obviously not a tape measure!"

"So, what could it . . . Oh. Oh, no way, Jon, no way!"

"What? What!?"

"We gotta get to my house! Now!"

"What are you talkin' about, Pete?"

"Jon," Pete pauses to take another drink of his iced tea, "I think I found it."

CHAPTER FOUR

At first I didn't believe him. I thought he was just joking or playing Abby's game of "ha ha, look at the great detective." But then, by analyzing his expression, I realize he was telling the truth. He had found it, or, at least he thought he had found it. What *it* was had yet to be determined.

We exit the oak, and head to Pete's house. He lives about a mile away, so it should not take that long to get there. I pick up my classic *Huffy*. It's not the best, but, it gets the job done. Mom picked it up for me at a yard sale a few years back.

Abby steps onto the back wheel's broken pegs and holds on while Pete gets on his electric scooter. He should really have a newspaper route with that thing.

The rumble of thunder, from an oncoming storm, looms in the distance. It's no surprise. It is in the mid 90's today and severe storms are in the forecast from now 'till Thursday.

With a nod of our heads we are off. No one says anything, but we are all aware that we have to make it there fast in order to beat the rain. Honestly I don't think any of us would mind the rain. We would even welcome it. It's just that being stuck outside in a downpour with a chance of getting struck by lightning, or even better, being caught in the path of a twister, is not on our "to do" list for the day.

Weaving in and out of parked cars and neighborhood kids playing street hockey, Pete does his best to beat us there. I give it my all, but with Abby weighing me down and decreasing my maneuverability, I don't have a chance to beat an electric scooter. I see an opportunity and pull a short cut through a small dog park. Abby taps me on the shoulder and points towards Pete on the other side. I reply by peddling as fast as I am able. I completely cross the park, dodge a properly pampered poodle and hop off the curb, landing right behind Pete. But this one is a win for him. Man, I almost had him too.

We roll up to his yard and Abby jumps off before I can come to a stop. I drop my bike in the front yard as Pete bolts around to the side of the house where he stores his scooter.

"I almost had you, Pete!"

"No, no, no. *Weeeee* almost had you, Pete," adds Abby.

"Ha ha. I know. Good thing too, I just now ran outta' juice." Pete reaches in to a large plastic storage box on the side of the house and pulls out one of those huge, orange, grounded extension cords. The same kind he uses to recharge his electric lawnmowers.

He's a real green freak. I guess he gets it from his dad who refuses to drive any car but an electric hybrid. Pete plugs the cord into the wall and attaches the other end to his scooter. He returns to the front of the house and waves us in.

Following Pete into his foyer, Abby and I say hello to his father, my uncle Rob. We remain unnoticed, however, because he is currently deep at work in his office building a scale replica of what appears to be the *USS Constitution.* That's how Pete and I got started with the hobby. Pete still builds one from time to time but I no longer have the patience for such a tedious task. Though, I must admit, Pete's models turn out amazingly, far better than the *Blackbird* in the oak. Uncle Rob's, however, are still "la crème de la crème!"

Pete's little brother, Jacob, sits in the neighboring room, deeply entrenched in his favorite first person shooter video game. His gaming tag is *GOML*, or "Get On My Level," which he frequently shouts at the TV screen after a successful headshot to one of his opponents. I used to play all the time but it seems like every month another company releases a new 60 dollar game and I just can't keep up.

"Come on, guys," Pete commands with a rush in his voice. Abby and I, back on track, follow Pete into his bedroom. He quickly shuts the door behind us and goes for his backpack which is hanging on his corner bedpost. He lays the bag on his bed and unzips the front pouch. He slowly pulls out a small, black, cylindrical object, presenting it to Abby and me, so we can inspect it for ourselves.

It is amazingly heavy for such a small object, about the size of a common remote control. Its smooth, perfect, metal surface is only interrupted twice, with two small screens that extend around the entire cylinder. There is a cover on the bottom, however. When removed, it reveals several buttons as well as a number pad. Underneath a separate cover is what appears to be a trigger of some sort. It stands alone and looks kind of important. I am unable to see any sort of compartment for batteries or a power source, however there are two types of input receivers that I am not familiar with.

"What do you think, Jon? That's got to be it, right? I mean . . . look at that thing. What else could it be?" Pete is right. This has got to be what they were all looking for.

"Where did you find this, Pete?" I ask.

"Ha! You'll never guess. I found it at the old plantation house! It was up against the corner of that old weathered stone wall on the northeastern corner."

"It was just lying there?" asks Abby, as skeptical as ever.

"Well, yeah, that's where it ended up." Pete says to Abby, who now, understandably, looks confused.

"Ya know how tall that grass was right? I mowed right over it! It scared the heck outta me! It's pretty indestructible considering it ricocheted around a couple times underneath the mower's carriage. The only damage it has is that little scrape on the side."

Pete points to the side as I rotate it. From what Pete says, it took quite a beating. But this scratch is so minute that I missed it on my first inspection.

"So what is it, guys?" asks Abby, a bit more interested and seemingly open-minded. She does tend to be the voice of reason in a lot of our escapades.

"It's not a digital tape measure, that's for sure," I say confident in my decree.

"And how are you so sure, Jon? Why can't it simply be a tape measure?

"I dunno, Abb. I mean, look. In theory it could be one I guess. It could be anything. But once again, why would they spend so much time, men and resources looking for a stupid tape measure," I ask emphatically. Just then, Pete interjects with, "Jonny's right! Just look at this thing: switches, numbers, screens, buttons, and slots. It's gotta be a dirty bomb or something! Remember what they were talking about? Some sort of thermal switch! Man, it's a weapon of some sort. I can feel it!"

As if on cue, lightning crashes outside and is quickly followed by a deep rumble of thunder. But there is still no rain, yet.

"Let's get back to the oak!" Pete says, worried about his little brother snooping as we no longer hear the ping pang of his video game.

I take the device, put it back into Pete's bag and throw it over my shoulder. We exit the bedroom and head to the front door, passing Uncle Rob, still meticulously working on his model. All three of us step outside and are greeted by a violent gust of wind. We get no farther than the front porch when out of the corner of my eye I spot the white van slowly creeping by us. The driver, Jackson, shoots me a cutting stare as we all freeze in our tracks. I panic and motion for all of us to return inside the house. The van comes to a halt.

Behind the curtain, from the front bay window, we peer outside, waiting for the van to continue on its way. Luckily for us, no one exits the van. It starts rolling down the street again as quickly as it stopped. To make sure the coast is clear, we wait a few minutes until the van is completely out of sight. Abby opens the door and gives a quick sweep of the road. The only vehicle in site is a rusty old yellow t-top, but it pulls into the garage, three doors down.

We exit Pete's house once again, round the corner and head towards our transportation. Pete gets his scooter and checks its battery gauge. This time he will have to walk. The gauge reads a 17 percent charge. Abby decides to walk as well. I follow her lead by guiding my bike and walking alongside it. We keep an ever vigilant, almost paranoid eye on every car that passes by. We make it back to the dog park and this time head down Maple Lane. It's a different route from how we came, but, depending on

41

the time of day, it's sometimes a short cut. With an impending storm, snooping goons, and traveling by foot, this shorter route was desperately needed.

We are abnormally quiet as we head back to the oak. My mind is a flutter with all of the device's possibilities and its true purpose, as well as the burden and wondering if we should involve anyone else. Is Pete right? Is it some sort of a bomb? If so, we would definitely have to involve our parents and the police. What about Abby? Could it really just be an expensive tape measure? Am I really reading too many comic books and my vivid summer vacation imagination was simply taking me away from reality? All these thoughts stream through my head as the first drops of rain fall from the sky.

"Jon! Look! The ice cream man," shouts Pete, breaking the eerie silence. In the distance, on the corner of Maple and Brattson, we see the ice cream man parked in his usual spot. No matter how old we get, ice cream is still ice cream. And come on, at any age, can you really beat ice cream being delivered right to your front door?

"I want a *Rainbow Blast* pop," cries Abby. It's amazing how fast our minds can switch from a possible nuclear bomb, to an ice cream cone. It's good to see that we are still hanging on to a bit of our youth.

"Ok, I guess we can all use it," I say. We are already wet. Might as well have some ice cream.

"Yeah and I'll treat. Today was plantation

42

pay day, baby!" Pete boasts as he pulls a wad of cash from his pocket.

Instead of making the next right onto Woodson, we continue down Maple to Brattson and aim for the ice cream man, who has since turned on his wipers and headlights due to the steadily increasing rain. Curiously, though, he is not playing his traditional dorky, yet whimsical melodies that he usually blasts throughout the neighborhood. I guess we just can't hear them yet with the thunder coming closer and closer.

I set my bike down as we approach the ice cream man's vehicle, still absent of the typical simple melodies. We begin to peruse the selection on the side of the vehicle. Abby cannot find her favorite *Rainbow Blast* pop listed and instead has to settle on strawberry, while Pete chooses chocolate. I am not as decisive. My taste buds have it narrowed down to *Cherry Berry Blast* and *Watermelon Whirler,* two flavors I have never heard of, but sound inviting, nonetheless. While viewing the pictures and prices, I notice that they are not painted onto the side panel as is customary. Instead, they are posted on the side of the ice cream van with magnetic posters, reminiscent of the ones that the lady with . . . Oh, no.

Just then the back of the van opens up and out pops four of the thugs from yesterday. The side door also slides open. Jackson looks up at me with a menacing grin. With a very rough voice he says, "Want some ice cream, kid?" This can't be happening. How could we, no, scratch that, how could *I* be so stupid? This is like *Hansel and Gretel* being lured to the gingerbread house to be cooked up as a tasty treat for the witch. But in this case, something tells me these guys had something else in mind.

"Run, you guys! Run!" I yell. As if on the cue of a firing pistol, we all take off as fast as we can. I go over to pick up my bike and hop on. I get one good thrust on the right pedal but am immediately stopped; one of the guys has reached out and snagged my back tire. He demonstrates his physical prowess by lifting the rear tire in the air while I am still on the bike. I quickly jump off, leaving my bike in the grasp of the behemoth and try to catch up to Pete and Abby who are now a good ten yards ahead of me. The heart of the storm has caught up to us now, pounding down with violent rain and wind, trumped only by the crash of thunder and lightning. I catch up to the others as we all run in the opposite direction of the van.

Rain during a competition, like a game of soccer, is supposedly to the benefit of the underdog. In this scenario, that couldn't be more wrong, giving more evidence to the fact that this is real and not a game at all. We are running, presumably for our lives, and we don't even know why. We simply know something wasn't, let's say, "Kosher," with this bunch. And now that we have their digital, bomb, thermal, tape measure . . . whatever it is, there is no stopping the men in their pursuit.

"Jonny! Where are we going, man? Where do we go?" Pete asks in a more than panicked manner. He is right. Where are we headed? I know the boss lady had to have seen me earlier in the oak and of course our pursuers just saw us at Pete's house.

"I dunno, dude, just keep running!"

Abby, who now leads the way, turns around and gives a facial expression that does not sit well with me. It's the same expression she had while watching a viral video of a car driving down the street, all quiet and calm until a skeleton man popped up and scared the "everything" outta us.

I turn around and see two of the guys giving chase: the guy who grabbed my bike as well as the stubby guy, Leo, from yesterday. The other two must have joined Jackson back in the would-be ice cream van, which was just now starting to move in our direction. At least, I hope that's where they are. Otherwise they may have taken a different route to intercept us. But where are we running to anyhow?

The rain is tremendous. I knew it was in the forecast but this is just ridiculous. I didn't know hurricane season started this early. I wonder if this tape measure thing can help us build an arc!

No time for jokes, though. We are losing ground. The men are catching up to us. They are so close that I can hear the stubby one talking to a female voice on his walkie talkie. It has to be the lady from yesterday.

"Jackson? Jackson?"

45

"Uh, no, ma'am, this is Leo . . . " he responds.

"What's going on? Did the kids have it? Did you get the temporal device?"

"In pursuit, ma'am, in pursuit . . . Gotta . . . gotta go now." This run was definitely not in the stubby man's job description.

I look at Pete as we both continue to run hard in the rain. He is puffing and panting as he should be. He already had his exercise for the day in mowing lawns. He looks back at me and nods. He knows what I'm thinking.

We round the corner and head towards the plantation house. Pete just mowed it, but he has nothing to do with the overgrown shrubs that border the entire yard. If we can make it there, we may be able to lose them, if not completely, but long enough to rethink our route.

Reaching the perimeter of the plantation yard, I throw the book bag over the overgrown boxwoods. We find the nearest break in the bushes and make sure Abby gets under cover first. She scurries underneath on her hands and knees. Pete and I are literally on her heels as we follow her through, dodging brush and branches. Abby smacks Pete in the face and splatters him with mud. Pete pauses to wipe his face but I quickly shove him through until we reach the other side. We pass a little squirrel also seeking shelter, but just from the rain. I am sure there are no evil squirrels chasing after him in search of his cherished stash of acorns.

We huddle behind the nearest shrubs in most need of pruning. I spot a cut on Abby's leg and ask if she is ok. She nods in approval as she looks down at her leg. She must have cut it on a thorn from one of the rose bushes that are haphazardly placed about boxwoods.

We sit in the pouring rain trying to catch our breath and composure. I realize that we have yet to recover Pete's bag since I threw it over bushes.

I look around and spot the backpack lying on a garden flagstone, behind Abby. Hugging the ground like a navy seal, I find my chance and crawl over and retrieve it. I unzip the front pocket and pull out the object. To my surprise, the interior of the pouch is illuminated with a red light. It is similar to the color of my alarm clock when I wake up in the middle of the night to let out Feebz.

I pull out the flashlight-shaped object to find it glowing in my hand. Somewhere between Pete's house and here, it had switched itself on. After chucking the bag over the shrubs, I guess I shouldn't be surprised. It could have landed on anything. Maybe the force of it hitting the flagstone turned it on or . . . I don't know.

Without saying a word, I present the item to Pete and Abby so they can inspect it for themselves. The source of the red light is now exposed; a series of numbers has appeared on the previously dimmed screens. The top row has a set of numbers, but each number keeps shifting on and off so we can't get a clear look at them all at once. Honestly, right now, I have no interest in what they represent since we are being chased in this wretched thunderstorm. The lower screen is more stable and I can make out the numbers: 1261941

Our wonderment of the device is short lived as we are alerted by the stomping feet of the men as they round the corner. We quickly quiet our breathing as if our life depends on it, which it very well might. There is no more communication on their walkie talkie. The only thing coming across now is static. They must be out of range or have too much interference due to the storm. The men look in our direction but I feel safe that they don't see us.

CHAPTER FIVE

As we watch them hunt for us like escaped slaves making our way north on the Underground Railroad, all I can think about is the device. I look down at it as I hold it in my hand. What is it? Why is it so special? And then it hits me. It may sound crazy but . . . but . . . of course! The lady on the walkie talkie, when she was checking in on her henchmen, referred to the object as a . . . oh, what was it . . . a "temporal" device. Temporal - dealing with space or time. Could it be? How could they lose something like that? I can't believe it! If it really is what I think it is, I simply can't believe it. I wish I could tell Pete and Abby immediately but we are still doing our best to imitate stone gargoyles, perched atop a Gothic cathedral in Europe.

Ever vigilant, we continue to watch the men through the tall hedges, shrubs and bushes. My heart races faster and faster as no doubt, theirs do as well. The men stand there, bothered, bewildered and as drenched as we are. The look of frustration and anger washes over their faces. They appear as if they are about to give up, or, I can only hope.

"AHHHH!" Abby screams wildly. I turn around to find Jackson with both hands on Abby's shoulders, dragging her away. He must have parked the van on the other side of the plantation house and crossed in through the back.

Pete and I get up to help free Abby from her assailant, as we know the other men will be here in no time. Abby, fighting back with all her might, spins around on the mud and is now looking right into Jackson's disturbing smirk. Before we can even get up to assist her, she leans backward, pumps her right leg back and then thrusts it into his left kneecap. Jackson falls to the ground in agony, cursing and spitting at Abby. He has to hate life right now. Abby has some pretty strong legs from all those years of playing soccer. She gets up and runs towards the front gate as Jackson lies on the ground wracked with pain.

The two men on the corner hear the chaos and violently tear through the hedges, making their way towards us. "Stop them!" shouts Jackson while still on the ground, gripped in agony. Pete grabs the device from my hand, shoves it back into his bag and throws it over his shoulder. "Come on!" he yells as we both take off towards Abby. Once again, she is in the lead as we all run across the enormous plantation property. As if having two men chasing us from behind wasn't bad enough - the van pulls up across the street. The remaining goons exit the van and enter the yard via a side gate. They are ready to join in on the chase and are now in full force. They cut us off from Abby as she keeps her heavy sprint towards the gate.

She makes her way to the other side of the lawn and to the main gate. She turns around to look for us. At the worst possible time, Pete clips the head of a shovel and takes a giant spill. The shovel had been overturned and submerged in a monster puddle next to a weed-filled flower garden. He takes a wild dive and slides across the lawn. His bag gets thrown from his shoulder and the device pops out. I rush over to quickly pull him up as he reaches for the device. Luckily, it did not get thrown that far and he easily recovers it. But it's too late. The two men are coming up behind us; the other two are headed straight at us. Jackson is now, miraculously back on his feet, limping this way. We are cornered.

The thugs, well aware that Pete and I have nowhere to run, slow their pace and wait for Jackson to reach them. The one who grabbed my bike earlier leans over and places his hands on his knees in an effort to catch his breath. Abby attempts to make her way back to us. She cautiously pauses, however, when I shake my head and wave her back. If we get caught, she is our only hope of getting help. She takes the cue, carefully backs up and hides behind a portion of the front gate. Jackson reaches his underlings as they close in on us.

Even though we are all completely drenched,

51

as if making a grand entrance to a fancy up-scale party, Jackson straightens his tie, adjusts his suit coat and takes his final, muddy steps toward us. Once again, lightning and thunder clap across the sky immediately above us, revealing the shiny chrome butt of a gun, sticking out from under Jackson's waist.

"Jon. Jon I'm scared, man! What do we do?" This is no joke and Pete knows it. We watch too many action movies and crime dramas on TV to know that this situation does not bode well for us.

"Ok, kids, no more fun and games. Hand it over," demands Jackson as he holds out his hand and motions for the device. Pete, always brazen at the most inappropriate time replies, "Forget you, man," while holding the object in plain view of the men, "We're not letting you have it. You just want to blow something up."

"Blow up something? Ha! What are you talkin' bout kid? It's a simple, uh . . . what did she call it again? A simple tape measure, that's all. Now just hand it over and we'll really get you your ice cream this time, ok?" Jackson explains.

"Ha, yeah, that's a good one, boss," says the stubby guy, an obvious sycophant of Jackson. The other men join in on the praise. Jackson loves every minute of it. With a few seconds of distraction, the only thing I can think of is . . .

"Pete. Pull the trigger!"

"What? Jon, are you crazy?"

"Lift the cover . . . and pull the trigger."
I whisper slowly to Pete.

"Dude, we will all blow up! Do you want me
to pull it, and then throw it? You think it's like, a
grenade or something? Is that what you want me to
do?"

"Peter, do you trust me?"

"Of course, man, but . . ."

"Then, pull the trigger. Right NOW!"

With the biggest expression of pain, conflict
and confusion, Pete looks at the device and then back
at me. I nod and mouth the words, "Do it." Pete holds
the device up and flips the trigger cover. This
movement attracts the attention of the praise-seeking
Jackson.

"Hey, kid! Don't touch anything on that, you
understand me?" Jackson insists. He pulls out his gun
and takes aim. But he is too late. Thank God Pete
pulls the trigger before Jackson.

CHAPTER SIX

A loud clap of anger and flash of light appear instantaneously. The sound is unlike the other crashes of thunder and lightning, however. It's as if a supersonic jet came out of nowhere, flew right above us and now is gone. I shudder back and forth as if a jolt of electricity has just run through my body. The tiny white hairs on my arms and legs stand up as the temperature rapidly increases and decreases. One second it's like a walk-in freezer and the next, it's like Death Valley. I feel as if I am floating, as if there is zero gravity. But then I am as heavy as ever, as if I just ran ten miles after eating Thanksgiving dinner.

All the sensations subside and for a minute I've obtained normalcy. Although, nothing is really normal, at all: the storm has stopped, the men are gone, and the plantation . . . everything is gone. Everything is different. I spot Pete lying beside me. It's a very comforting feeling to see a familiar face even though he looks a bit more dazed and confused than I.

"Jon. Oh, man. Oh, man are we dead, dude? I blew us up! Why did you tell me to pull it? I trusted . . ."

"Calm down, Pete. We're not dead. At least, I'm pretty sure we're not dead." I explain.

"Well, if we're not dead, this is most definitely heaven on Earth, dude! Look around! It's amazing!" says Pete.

"I know. I know," I say, trying to take it in and make sense of it all.

Our neighborhood has been replaced by a wide open, lush, tropical landscape. We are in a valley surrounded by mountains to what I assume is the east and west of us. There are wild flowers and exotic looking birds all over the place. It's perfect here, a veritable Utopia. No wonder Pete called it Heaven.

"Well I don't know where we are Jon, but for real, I'm just glad we're alive. Those guys were out for blood! Did you see that gun? I mean, what is this thing anyways?" Pete looks under and all around him, but has no luck finding it.

"Where is it Pete?"

"I don't know, I just had it, I mean . . . I just pulled the trigger thing, ya know? You saw me! It's gotta be around here somewhere."

"True." I agree as we search our surroundings.

"And, Jon, um . . . what is it? Is it like a teleporting gun or something that like, beamed us up

55

or something? I mean, you told me to push it, so you must have known it wasn't a bomb, right? Right? Dude, please tell me you were totally sure it wasn't gonna blow us up, Jonny!"

"I was pretty sure," I admit and smile up at Jon.

"Bad form, man! That would have been an epic fail, for the both of us!" Pete shakes his fist at me. "So what is it then?"

"Pete, when they were chasing us did you catch anything coming across their walkie talkie?"

"Yeah, it sounded like that hot chick from the Jaguar and she called it a . . . um . . . temp, tempra, temprational . . ."

I have to stop him. He sounds like an idiot. School is out and there is no sense of watching him torture himself as well as the English language.

"Temporal, Pete, temporal. She called it a temporal device. It means: of or pertaining to time and space.

"Temporal! Yeah, like in that video game my brother got last week, *The Temporal Travelers*. It's where this police detective goes back it time to help solve unsolved cases and then he . . . Wait. Jon, are you saying what I think you're saying?

"Yup. We just traveled through time, buddy."

I pause and think; we traveled through time. Suddenly my mind is full of all sorts of possibilities, scenarios, concepts, causes and effects. Where are we? In what time period: the past, present, future?

Why was this destination programmed into the device? How do we get back home? Even still, *can* we get home? But none of the questions matter right now. We no longer had that crazy gadget.

I intensify my search and instruct Pete to do the same. "Pete, we need to find that thing. It's not a matter of life or death, but a matter of living here or our normal lives back at home." Pete expands his search and jogs over to a trio of palm trees about fifty yards away. I go in the opposite direction towards the closer of the two mountain ranges. The sun is hot and bright but there is a cool wind rushing through the valley.

And there, in the distance, a bit more to the south, I can see the shore. Wow. Did we really end up on some deserted island? I sure hope we're not in the Jurassic period. If the recent flicks from Hollywood have anything right about dinosaurs, Pete and I have no chance at all at surviving out here. I walk a bit more and approach an abrupt precipice. I gingerly approach the ledge and look down. The cliff rises about 100 feet above the land below. There is what appears to a gravel road underneath. My worry about Velociraptors quickly dissipates.

"Jonny! Jonny!" shouts Pete from about a football field length away. "I think I found it!" I rush over to the patch of palms and see Pete reaching down as if to pick something up, hopefully the device.

"You got it, Pete?"

57

"Yeah. Look," Pete says while holding the time gadget. Once again, the only flaw on it is the scratch that we saw before. All the numbers are present now on both displays. The upper screen has around 13 different numbers. I still have no clue what they represent.

"That was easy," Pete says, rather matter of factly.

"Yeah," I say, "compared to Jackson and his crew, that is. They must have been so frustrated not being able to find it. But look, we landed, um, we, arrived, whatever you want to call it. We arrived in an open area. They lost it in our neighborhood. I wonder how long they were searching for it?"

"Couldn't have been that long, Jon. I just mowed that lawn not too long ago, ya know?"

"True, true. It's no wonder why they were so ticked off ya know, man?"

"Ha ha. Especially when they were taking orders from the Jaguar lady! I mean she is one fly mama, but I could see her cracking the commands on those guys, ya know? She meant business, Jon."

Suddenly, from over a ridge behind us, the roars of several engines interrupt our conversation. We immediately turn around and are faced with three old-school looking jeeps, trudging across the landscape. "Wow!" Pete mutters under his breath. "Wherever and whenever we are, we didn't go back that far at all," I insist. The three jeeps follow each other in a single file line until they reach us when they spread out and surround us as much as they are able. Just before the jeeps come to a final stop, I take the device and stick it in my right side pocket, hoping and praying that it will not be discovered.

The jeeps are painted in the standard olive drab military green. The sides are decorated with a white star insignia and the words U.S. ARMY. I am feeling safer by the second. Each jeep has two men, a driver and a passenger. The passenger of the lead jeep, my height, about mid forties, steps out and asks, "You boys lost?" We stand here, dumbfounded, turn and stare at each other, not having a clue how to respond.

"Um, yes, sir. We were just, umm," Pete has no clue where he is going with this.

"Just a little far off from the beach, aren't we," asked the, what I presume to be a general or sergeant at least. He has a ton of stripes and other designations on his uniform.

"Yes, sir." I agree. "We were just going for a hike but got turned around a bit and have been lost for a while now."

"We'll take you back, ok boys? You two took quite a little hike, didn't you? Your folks are probably worried sick."

"Ha, yeah, thank you, sir." I nod in agreement.

"You can ride with us," the GI says as he opens the mini door to his jeep. We walk over to the vehicle and hop up into the back seat, adjusting for the two duffle bags that are already there. The driver starts the engine and we are on our way headed down the hill. We meet up with the gravel road that I saw earlier. It soon turns into a more permanent, paved road.

"So, where are you boys staying? We're headed back to Wheeler and . . ."

"Wheeler?" I interrupt.

"Yes, Wheeler Airfield," he replies.

"Sir, are we anywhere near Schofield, Hickam, or . . ." I take big gulp of air, "Pearl?"

"Yeah, kid, we sure are. All of them. You're pretty smart for a tourist. Your father military?"

"No, no." I reply. "I am, uh, I am just thinking about enlisting in a couple years," I finally get the words out." It really wasn't a lie. I had thought about joining some branch of the service, but not now, not here. Why didn't I think about it earlier? Those numbers weren't random at all. It's all coming together now.

"Well that's good, son. And who knows, what with all that's goin' on across the globe now-a-days, we're gonna need all the help we can get. I don't know how long we can sit around and watch our friends across that mighty pond get their butts whooped, ya know, kid?" the soldier said, while slowly and emotionally wiping the sweat from his brow.

"Waikiki is a bit out of our way, but that'll be no problem. Where are you boys staying anyways?"

"Waikiki?" I ask, still in disbelief.

"Yeah, you know, Honolulu, the beach! What hotel are you champs staying at?"

"Uh, ummm," I mutter. "The old one."

"The old one, ay? Well, you're gonna have to narrow it down a bit. The oldest one is the *Moana Surfrider*, that sound familiar?

"The big pink one," Pete shouts while winking at me.

"Oh," the soldier says, "the *Royal Hawaiian*. That's a very nice one! I love that new drink they got there. They named it after Shirley Temple, since she stays there so often. That cute 'lil darling. That drink is the cat's meow."

"Yes, sir," says Pete as we continue down the road. We pick up speed and the conversation stops due to the amount of wind all around us. The open top of the jeep is a blessing for me and Pete. If we had to talk anymore the soldiers would definitely know something was up and that we were more than their average tourist.

We drive for about ten minutes. The two other jeeps that were following pass us as we near Wheeler Airbase. Our jeep speeds up as we merge onto a larger highway. It's so windy it reminds me of my sailing trip a few years back with Grandpa.

Out of nowhere, two fully armed P-40 Warhawks rumble across the sky and fly directly above us. Pete and I have a model of one in our treehouse. I feel like I am at an air show with my

61

family but the only difference is, well, this is the real deal.

"Those are Warhawks, boys," the soldier shouts back at us, competing against the wind.

"They look like they are from WWII," declares Pete as I quickly punch his shoulder as hard as I can. He gives me a surprised look, but somehow knows, that he was in the wrong by saying that.

"Too windy, can't hear ya, boys," The soldier yells back. Thank God he didn't hear Pete. I have to explain the situation to Pete as soon as I can.

CHAPTER SEVEN

We drive for about a half an hour more and pull up to this gigantic pink hotel, just as Pete described. I guess I have to give him credit for this one. The soldier steps out and we follow.

"Ok, boys, you're on your own now. Stay on the beach, okay!" The soldier chuckles as he walks back to the jeep. I am able to hear him say something under his breath, to his driver: "Kids and their clothes now a days."

Uh-oh. We'd better find some clothes quick.

The jeep drives away and we wave goodbye. Pete and I turn and face the enormous hotel. It reminds of me of the grandiose hotels on the Vegas strip. Not that I've ever been there, but I have seen them in movies enough times to know how amazing they are.

Tourists and locals both hustle and bustle in front of the hotel and the surrounding area. A man and woman in their twenties hold hands while walking towards the beach which lies beyond a little stone path. The woman is wearing a one piece swim suit that is something my grandmom would wear. It leaves everything to the imagination. The guy on the other hand, well, let's just say you would not ever catch me wearing that swimsuit in public. It basically looks like the type my school swim team wears. However, this guy has his pulled up almost as high as his belly button.

The guy looks over at us and gives a look up and down. He nudges the women to look over and she giggles. With those swimsuits on, I can't believe *we* are the ones that are dressed funny.

"Jon, are you gonna tell me what's up? You know where we are, don't you? I mean I know were in Hawaii but . . ."

"Yeah, that was a good one back there, the pink hotel and all. How did you know, Pete?"

"'Cuz I came here last summer with Bobby Newton and his family. This is where we stayed. Although, not everything is the same. So, I know were in Hawaii but, I mean, look at all these classic cars, man. It's amazing! Is it the fifties?"

"Hold on, Pete. You're right, were in Hawaii. But those aren't classic cars. And this isn't just anytime to visit Hawaii."

"Nice! Is it an awesome surf competition or something? We missed one last year and I'd love to catch one now."

"Ha ha, I'll explain it all man, but we gotta get out of these clothes. We need to blend in."

"Woah! Woah, Jon! I am not wearing what that guy was wearing!"

"Yeah, I don't blame you. Look!"

Rounding the corner of the hotel was a native islander, pushing around a giant linen cart. She must be a member of the hotel's maid service. She pushes the cart up to the side, looks at her watch, and leaves the cart behind. Break time perhaps? Pete and I tiptoe over in her absence. "This is just what we need," I tell Pete.

The bin is filled with clothes. It must be a laundry service or something. The hotel is a pretty upscale place, perhaps for celebrities and such. It doesn't surprise me that they take care of their guests' laundry.

"*This* is what we need?" Pete asks while holding up a bra. "Just dig deeper," I tell him. I pull out a shirt and some shorts and then another shirt. Pete's too busy, still entertaining himself with the bra as he places it over his chest and gives me a feminine wave. I shout at him and tell him to, "find some clothes, now!" He drops the bra and pulls up a pair of socks. We continue digging until we find our blend-in outfits; they are not our ideal look but will have to do. Anything was better than my "I Survived the Beast Express," shirt, referring to a ride in an amusement park that I am sure doesn't yet exist. Pete's most recent *Ripped Rock Tour* shirt will not work either.

We take cover behind the linen cart and switch into our new clothes. I carefully remove the device and stick it in my new pair of pants. We look up at each other and bust out in laughter. "We look like one of those fake antique photos that you get made on the boardwalk, Jon!"

We do look ridiculous. And who knows if we are even wearing this stuff in the style that it's being worn? We start to walk towards the beach as the sun begins to set in front of us. I point to a wooden bench and Pete and I take a seat. Two boys, a little younger than us, cross our path and continue to walk back towards the pink hotel. Their clothes are just like ours. The only difference is their socks are pulled all the way up.

"You see that, Jon?"

"Yup, sure did."

"Guess we gotta pull'em up! Okay. So now can you tell me what's goin' on?"

I slowly and carefully pull the object from my back pocket, shielding it from the nearby tourist traffic and show it to Pete. I point to the numbers on the screen, the same ones from before. They meant nothing to me then, back at his house, but it's so obvious now.

"Ok, Pete, so we know we are in Hawaii, right?"

"Yeah."

"And we know it's not in our time, right?"

"Ha, yeah, man. I'm glad too. I would never be able to last in these clothes," Pete says as he points to his newly acquired shorts being held up by a giant blue button. "So what is this, Jon, the twenties or something? I mean, look at my clothes, dude!"

"Not that far back, Pete."

"The sixties?"

"Ha ha. No, no, the forties. Look at the display. It reads 1261941. We're in the year 1941, Pete. December 6, 1941, to be precise. Aaaaaannndddd were in Hawaii. Mean anything to you?"

"Uhhh is a volcano about to erupt or something, cuz if it is . . ."

"Pete!

"Look, Jon, I like history and all but I'm not a fanatic about it like you. Just tell me!"

"Pete . . . Hawaii, 1941, come on, bro!"

"Jon, I don't know, just tell . . .wha . . . 1941? Hawaii, 1941? Oh, my . . . Oh, my God, save us. Are you serious, man? You mean the Bay of Pigs is about to be attacked?

"PETE!"

"Ha ha! Just playing, bro. Pearl Harbor! Pearl Harbor! I know. Honestly though, that is wild. It's tonight right?"

"No, no. We still have a little bit of time. It's not until tomorrow morning, Sunday, December 7, 1941. For some reason the time device was set to the day before the attack. But I don't know why."

"Curious, dude. Very curious." Pete replies, looking perplexed.

Why here and why now? What were they planning? Why would anyone want to go back to

Pearl Harbor the night before the bombing? Did they just want to see the bombing of Pearl Harbor, to be silent observers in a part of American history? Or was it a more sinister motive. Well, since they were armed and chasing us I am going to have to go with the latter. But nothing can be more sinister than the surprise attack itself. I just don't know.

As I sit on the bench, staring at the date on the screen, still pondering why it would be set to this date, it shuts off. The display date is gone. In its place is a tiny green light, one I didn't notice before. It starts flashing on and off. There is no label or tag or anything else on it. I ask Pete what he thinks it is, even though I know he has no more clue than I.

"I dunno, Jon, maybe a light that tells you when the batteries are dying?"

"Batteries!" Geez! I had never thought about that. What was powering this thing anyway and what would happen if it ran out of juice. Would we be stuck here forever? Too bad we don't have a scientist inventor to help guide us along the way.

Speaking of scientists, I wonder if they started the Manhattan Project yet. I can't quite remember when they initiated it. But I do remember Einstein's letter was sent to Roosevelt in 1939, to inform him of the capabilities of a bomb.

"Man, too bad we don't have Einstein with us now. If anyone would know how to work this thing, it would be him," I tell Pete.

"Yeah, man. He would be a big help right

about now. Or even one of those crazy, German scientists. I remember watching a documentary in class last year about all these wild inventions the Nazis were trying to make and sometimes, succeeded in making!"

"Really? Like what?" I ask Pete, in both a curious and somewhat mocking fashion.

"Oh, the Japanese had some crazy ones too! Like these things called fuegos, or like . . . oh, man, what were they, like, these balloons sent up from Japan that would fly over to the West coast of the US and were used to start fires."

"I remember hearing something about that too, incendiaries right, Pete?"

"No, they were just supposed to set things on fire."

"Yeah, I know that's an inc . . . never mind, Pete."

"The US military even had something called Project X-Ray! They would take these bats they rounded up from caves in Texas, strap tiny, little bombs on them, put them in canisters and then drop them on Japan. Some crazy ideas back then, or . . . I mean, right now, ha ha."

"Nice," I smile and reply.

"The Nazis had some of the wildest ones though."

"Like what, Pete?" I am actually becoming interested now. After all, we are in possession of a pretty crazy invention, ourselves.

"Like this sound cannon thing that would shoot out these sound waves that immobilized you. Can you imagine being killed by sound? That would suck."

"Yeah that would be the end of a bad day. You wouldn't even see it coming."

"They even did some experiments on time travel. Wild stuff! But, then again, we just time traveled so, I guess it's not so wild after all."

"Yeah!"

We both sit and think. It was still sinking in. We had gone back in time. It was ridiculous to think of such a thing, but I mean, look at all the other things Man has accomplished through the years. It was only a matter of time I guess - pun intended.

What were we supposed to do? One of the most important events in American, no, scratch that, in *World* History was about to take place, and a deadly event at that. We are the only ones around who know what's coming.

"So what are we gonna do, Jon? Are we gonna stop it from happening?

"No. No way, Pete, not at all."

"You are, of course, joking right? Do you really want to see all of these people die . . . including us, possibly?"

"It's not that, Pete. It's simply . . ."

Just then I get slammed in the face with something. It was fairly light and didn't hurt at all but certainly caught me off guard. I look behind the bench and see the culprit: a beach ball. "Sorry! So sorry," a voice comes from the distance. It's a little girl with her father. They both jog our way. "Sorry, son," says the man.

"It's ok, sir. No problem at all." Staying seated, I rotate and lean over, retrieving the ball. I scoop it up and hand it back to the little girl.

"Thanks, mister," she replies.

"Guess it got away from us," the father says.

"Ha, yeah that always used to happen to my dad and me when I was her age," says Pete. I would hit the beach ball as hard as I could and make my dad go chase after it, ha ha!"
The man laughs. "Well, not when you were her age, she's only seven."

"Yeah, that's 'bout right," Pete confirms.

"Well these things were just introduced a few years back and I doubt you're only ten years old, son!"

"Oh . . . oh, yeah, I mean it was a football or something, haha." Pete does his best.

"Okay, take care boys." The father turns to his daughter and says, "It's getting dark, let's get back to the hotel, dear," as they walk away on the sand covered sidewalk.

Pete looks up at me, raises his eyebrows and hands at the same time. It is his way of saying he's sorry for yet another time-traveling blunder. We again sit down on the bench overlooking the beach in front of us. The silhouettes of two seagulls squawk in front of the final bits of daylight that struggle to hang on. I must tell Pete about time travel and all of its absurdity.

"Pete, that was blunder number two, dude."

"Jonny, I know. I'm sorry, bro. How was I to know that beach balls were just invented? It's not like it's a personal robot butler or something! It's just a dumb inflatable colorful ball!"

"I know, man, but just remember, 1941, ok? Just for our own safety and to remain as inconspicuous as possible, just assume . . . I dunno, just, assume nothing is invented yet or things haven't happened yet or, or . . . I dunno, just be careful!

"Alright, alright, sorry!"

"Just a few basics, ok, Pete? WWII is happening in Europe but the US doesn't enter it until the day after tomorrow. That's when President Roosevelt, Franklin, not Teddy, will ask congress for a declaration of war. So that's that. There is no rock-n-roll, radios are the most entertaining things in the average family household and, and, and . . ."

"Slow down, professor, I think I missed some of the notes," Pete says in a stereotypical nerdy voice, followed by another chuckle.

"Dude, I mean it, this is serious! I mean, Hawaii is not even a state yet, ok?

"Shut up? For real? Wow, really? What is it then!"

"A territory, but listen, Pete . . ."

"Hey, I got one! You know who are not

72

people yet? Us! Ha ha ha ha!"

"PETER! Enough!" I shake my head in disbelief. And this one is important!"

"Alright, alright. Have at me, mate," he says in a cockney accent.

"We have to do our best not to interact at all."

"Seriously, Jon? We have only been here like an hour and we've already gotten a ride in a US ARMY jeep, took clothes from a hotel maid, got laughed at by a couple and got hit in the head with a beach ball! How can we be here and not interact?" Pete asks, as frustrated and confused as ever.

He was actually right. The only way we could not interact is if we were invisible. I can't believe we had already broken the cardinal rule of time travel.

"Ok, that's true. But any little thing we do, any little thing at all, may change the future."

"Well, not anything, Jon, I mean, like, who cares if we got hit in the head with that beach ball."

"*I* got hit in the head, not you, Mr. Lucky. That's probably true. But take those army guys for example. They weren't supposed to pick us up. We weren't here in 1941. What if they were supposed to be somewhere else? What if they die tomorrow in the attack and missed out on being with their families for even a little bit longer. Or the clothes we took. Someone is missing their clothes, now. What if it's for some child actor and he doesn't have his clothes.

73

Now he misses his audition, an audition that would propel him into entertainment history, forever! But now he is late for the audition, misses the opportunity, gives up the acting life and ends up sleeping on the beach every night! And now he doesn't meet his wife and doesn't have kids and they don't have great-grandkids and their one great, great grandson who was going to find the cure for cancer will never be born! See what I'm getting at, Pete?

Pete shakes his head and says, "Whoa, that's sick, man. I would hate to be responsible for any of that. But ya never know, maybe things would work out for the better! Ya think?"

"We can't take that chance, Pete. Everything is connected. Someone we meet may impact the whole world's future. We just have to be observers as much as we can. Cool? Agreed?"

"Ok gotcha, Jon. Dude, we're gonna be stuck here forever."

The little green light increases its speed and is now flashing faster and faster. It's just another reminder that we know nothing about this thing. I turn it around and reveal the keypad. I start pushing the numbers hoping that the date screen, as well as the other numbers, reappears. But I have no luck at all. I don't want to mess with it too much in fear of wherever else it would send us, other than home. I mean, granted, being on the island of Oahu the night before the Japanese attack is bad enough, but I can only imagine it could have sent us to many other worse times and places.

I give up messing with the keypad and glance over at Pete. His reality is finally sinking in. His eyes are watering and he is doing his best to keep his tears at bay. That's how he is. As close as we are, he still thinks it's childish if he opens up and cries. But I know Pete. The best way to snap him out of it is to change the subject and not talk about it. I reach over with my right arm and pull his head down and give him the hardest noogie ever.

"Stop, Jon, Stop!" He laughs.

"Come on, man. Let's do some sightseeing. This is *my* first time in Hawaii, remember?"

"But, Jon, what if I mess up again?" he asks as he sniffles.

"Come on," I jab him in his side, "You'll be fine!"

"Well, Old Chap," he says, once again in his cockney accent, "Let me show ya a bit of the Waikki of old!"

We get up from the bench and head towards the lights of downtown, while repeatedly saying, "'Ello, Guvna!"

CHAPTER EIGHT

Ok, so we look the part, now we just have to do our best to act the part. And this is the place alright, downtown Honolulu. Wow! Even in the forties this place is as busy as can be. People are all over the main street, walking, talking, eating and shopping. It's as if the beach doesn't exist and is just an added bonus. All these people care about is the night life. And I can't blame them. It's the same back in the present. Every summer, my folks and I, as well as Pete and his family, rent this huge beach house in Myrtle Beach, South Carolina. It's amazing! We are on the beach all day and then drive around to see the sites at night. I guess some things don't change. And why would they?

A massive yellow station wagon, completely paneled in wood, drives by us. Strapped to the roof are these three big hunks of wood, each about 10-12 feet long; The forties' rendition of surfboards I'm guessing. They must weigh a good 300 pounds each!

"Look what we have here, chap: primitive specimen of coffee tables strapped to the top of an old Woody!" Pete had not yet lost his cockney accent.

"Ha ha! I think those are actually surfboards, Pete."

"Oh, ok!" He quickly loses the English brogue. "But I know I'm right about the Woody part!"

"Oh, yeah?" I doubtingly ask.

"Yes, sir. My lil' bro just finished a model of one of them last month! I'll bet you *Crusaders of Virtue,* issue one that it's a Ford"

"Ok, Pete, I'll take that bet." It could be anything: Pontiac, Chevy. But even if I lost, he already knows I have two copies of that first issue. I bought a used copy at a yard sale. I won the other one from Abby when she bet me I wouldn't go up to Principal Rasspy's house, dressed as a Girl Scout, selling cookies, door to door. I know I made a fool of myself and well, Principal Rasspy never looked at me the same way again, but it got me that first issue, and it was in a lot better condition than my other one.

The wood paneled car pulls up to the intersection awaiting the go ahead from the traffic signal. This gives us a chance to get a closer look. We both scan it over looking for the symbol, but no luck. There is no familiar blue logo, hood ornament, emblem or anything distinguishable at all. But that doesn't deter Pete.

"Hey, bud, nice hotrod!" he shouts to the driver.

Pete, everybody's friend, even in the 1940s, was not about to lose this bet that easily. One of the four male occupants leans out of the passenger door and replies, "Thanks, kid. Its killer diller! Better than that old jalopy over there!" he says as he points to the car on the opposite side of the street.

"Um, yeah, yours is the dog's bark!"

"Huh? The dog's . . . Oh! I like it! I like it! I never liked saying the 'cat's meow' anyway!"

"Ha, It's a Ford, right?" Pete asks, hoping to win the bet.

"Come on, Harry, we gotta get going!" exclaims a guy in the back seat.

"Sorry, boys. My friend is a little doll dizzy! Gotta go meet some girls at the theatre! And yeah, it's a Ford!" he replies as the Woody wagon pulls off and heads down the street.

"That was awesome, Jonny!" I nod my head in agreement. It *was* a really nice car. Too bad those were the only cool station wagons that came out of Detroit. One of Abby's neighbors drives a station wagon from the eighties. It has classic license plates on it but trust me, it's no classic. What a failed attempt at replicating the wood panels of earlier wagons. It doesn't do any justice to the original that we just saw in all its cruising glory.

"I want that mint issue that you won off of Abby too, not that crappy other one, Jon!

"Hey now. That was not part of the bet!"

"We probably won't make it back anyhow."

Pete frowns as his head droops towards the ground.

"Hey, don't talk like that, dude! Come on, what did I say?" I take a long pause.

"Okay, you can have the mint copy, but chin up alright, bud?" All this talk about Abby has me wondering about home as well.

"Yeah. Hey, Jon, they were headed to the movie theatre. I think I know which one too!"

"How can you know?"

"Because when I was here last year we went to it, it's still up today, I mean, in our day and it's like the oldest one around. It's gotta be the same one! Let's go!

"Cool. I bet you there's just gonna be some dumb boring old movie showing, but alright."

It was a good idea for a few reasons: it would keep our mind off of things, it would keep us from slipping up and it would keep us safe, for at least a few hours. I look down the street and see the Woody make a left turn. Pete and I head down along the sidewalk. He keeps stopping every ten steps to pull up his socks. I guess we should have kept digging for a tighter fit.

Several girls come out of a music shop on the left. Their socks, unlike ours, are a lot shorter. Although they are nothing like the crew or athletic, bootie socks of our time, they sure do look more comfortable than ours. "Forget this." I hear Pete yell as he lets his socks flop down to his shoes. Honestly, I am about to take mine off, too.

79

We continue walking amongst the hustle and bustle of old school Hawaiian night life, bumping into tourists, locals, and enlisted men on leave for the evening. As we get closer to the heart of the city more and more stores have tinsel and garland strewn across their storefronts and windows. Being in the past, being in Hawaii and being so close to the attack on Pearl Harbor, I guess I forgot that it was December.

We pass a toy store where a giant skyscraper erector set towers around an equally impressive plastic molded Santa, waving his arm up and down. We briefly pause and glance in at the antiquated display. A boy around age five and his mother approach the window and join in on our wonderment. He points at an erector set built as a train engine and says, "Mommy, Mommy, I'm going to ask Santa for this one!"

I think about what the boy has just said. Everything is going to change for him and his mom, for Hawaii, for America, for the world. I want to unleash a waterfall of tears, but I uncharacteristically hold it back for the benefit of Pete. He needs me more now than ever.

I wish we could warn them, could tell the whole town, could skip tomorrow all together. I wish we could prevent all the deaths that the whole war would bring to America and the world. But alas, we can't. It had already happened. Who were we to change it? The history books were written. WWII happened for a reason. I can't say why exactly but, perhaps if we didn't have WWII we wouldn't have learned any lessons from it. Perhaps a later war, when more countries had nuclear technology, would have been so much more deadly. Trying to interfere in the slightest would be a major disruption and who knows what kind of changes it would create for everyone's future.

"Ok, Billy, remember to add it to your list so we can mail it to the North Pole," the mother cheerfully replies. I briefly snap out of the conundrum of time travel and am put back into the happiness and joy that is Christmas. It's weird really: palm trees and shorts along with tinsel and garland. I am accustomed to cold temperatures in December. Then again, being in 1941 is just a bit more strange that a warm-weathered Christmas.

We continue to head down the street, following the same path as the Woody. We already lost sight of it but we're pretty sure of which street it turned on. We pass a giant alley, but instead of being dark and empty, it is filled with a ton of white tents and huts in what appears to be huge flea market. Both of us, taken in by the racket and accompanying excitement, decide to take a stroll through the packed side street.

Before we enter the market, we pass by a newspaper stand, the kind that is rare nowadays, except in bigger cities. Surprised to see that it's still open at this hour, we both walk up to the stand. A scruffy looking guy, in his mid thirties or so, sits back behind it, his head being propped up artificially with his hands as he reclines and rests his feet upon the backside of the counter top. He looks up at us, briefly, and uninterested, shuts his eyes. I guess he doesn't have many young customers on a daily basis.

Pete and I simultaneously reach for the copy of the *Honolulu Star Bulletin*. We read the date. Sure enough, it's December, 6, 1941. I mean, we were both already convinced that it was true, but nothing says it more than being written down on a daily newspaper. Tomorrow's paper would be the famous, or rather, infamous one, announcing the bombing. Shortly thereafter Hawaii will be placed under martial law. Just another grim reminder of the events about to unfold.

We weave in and out of tables that display all sorts of unique trinkets and souvenirs. The table peddlers are doing their best to gain our attention. They must do a great business in the heart of the city with all the tourists willing to spend some cash on their short, but memorable visits. The tables have a variety of local handcrafted, native items as well as your usual, typical souvenirs that can be found at any tourist trap, complete with the destination's name written in large letters. In this case, "Welcome to beautiful Hawaii."

We pass one table featuring hand carved surfboards, miniature bronze statues of aloha dancing girls dressed in grass skirts as well as palm tree lamps. I stop at the table and admire the craftsmanship of the hand carved items. "Jon, check this out!" Pete exclaims. He motions over to a neighboring table that is full of one thing only, ukuleles. Pete and I both love music and started taking guitar lessons when we were in middle school. We are both pretty good, but he has pursued it a bit more than I have. Once we entered high school, my courses sort of took over my life.

Pete picks up a ukulele and starts plucking it while shaking his hips, imitating some of the little dancing girl statues on the adjacent table.

"Stop, man, ha ha!" I bust out with a much needed laugh. I can't take his dancing and clowning around. He knows this fact, so he just increases the show. Some tourists stop their shopping and began to cheer him on. Great! All we need now is to draw more attention to ourselves. But I can't stop him. And why should I? He's in the moment and we both need a good laugh.

After a few more minutes of Pete in the spotlight, the local guy, manning the booth, finally comes over and says, "You gonna buy that, right, kid?" which stops Pete on the spot. He puts the ukulele down and the show is over. The audience briefly chuckles at Pete's reaction and gives a comical round of applause. Pete takes a bow and in his best, for some reason, Spanish accent, says, "Gracias, amigos, gracias! I take tips! I take tips!"

We head through the rest of the tables and

pass more anxious vendors to the left and right of us. "Dude, that was awesome! Did you see that, Jon! They loved me!"

Pete was right. They did love him and, although it totally went against everything we had to do to remain inconspicuous, we both needed it, indeed.

"I know! You rocked! You should form a band, dude," I encourage.

"Ha ha, ya think? That was more acting than anything else," Pete chuckles.

Pete reaches into his pocket and pulls out a crisp twenty dollar bill from his wad of today's earnings.

"It was only five bucks! I should have bought it." He holds the twenty up and waves it in the air.

"Yeah, Pete, but that twenty was probably made in the twenty-first century." Pete brings it down from his hand and takes a closer look.

"Two thousand three. Yup, you're right again, Jonny Boy!"

As soon as Pete finishes his sentence, I feel a tap on my back. An older lady in traditional Hawaiian dress steps a bit too close for comfort and says, "Young man. Young man, is that item for sale?" I guess she mistakes me for a table vendor. She points behind me but the tables are all in front of us.

"I'm sorry, ma'am I don't work here. I don't have a table with items or anything for sale like that."

84

"Not on a table, young man, in your back pocket. That item with the blinking green light. What is it? Is it for sale my young friend?

This chick is creeping me out. She was not the sweet old-lady grandma type either, but more like the evil witch in every fairy tale Mom read as she tucked me into bed.

"Oh, no. No sorry, uh, that's not for sale." She grabs me as if to turn me around for a closer look, but I resist, which is no challenge at all.

"Please, young man, show me what it is, please. I bet my grandson would love it for Christmas. Is it some kind of new toy or is it a green flashlight or . . . ?"

"It's a flashlight, just a flashlight! Gotta go!" I grab Pete and we take off running to the end of the alley towards the adjacent street.

"Shove that deeper in your pocket," insists Pete.

"Yeah, man. Good idea."

We continue up a street named Bethel and see the glowing lights of the theatre up ahead. A massive crowd lines up along the front of the building. The glow of the neon lights is striking as it surrounds the theatre's title, simply named, "Hawaii." If this theatre was out in the open, you could see its lights for miles. It obviously is a showpiece of downtown Honolulu.

The marquee off to the side reads:

NOW PLAYING:
DR JEKYLL and MR HYDE
STARRING SPENCER TRACY
INGRID BERGMAN and
LANA TURNER

"Yup, just where I left it," Pete jokes, remembering his visit from last year.

"What movie did you see here last year?"

"Oh, we didn't see anything actually. I wanted to see *Revenge of the Vampires III* but Mom was all like . . . 'No, no. We have better things to do while were in Hawaii.'"

"So what did you do in place of the movie?" I ask.

"Um, it was kinda cool to be honest. We went to the *Dole* Pineapple plantation."

"Oh, whatcha do, pick pineapples?" I laugh.

"Ha, no, man. They have this amazing maze. It's like the biggest in the world or something. It took me forever to find my way out. I ended up having to cheat and climb on the shoulders of this one guy who had two little kids. He was lost too and his kids were crying so we worked together. Oh, yeah, they had these chocolate covered pineapples and this train and . . . ya know what? First thing I do when we get back to our normal time is thanking my mom for not letting me see the vampire movie that day!"

"Yeah, man. Right on." I agree while giving

86

him a high five.

We notice that the guys from the Woody are waiting in line at the theatre. The guy that was in a rush to leave is now excessively flirting with a girl waiting outside of a phone booth. I guess that's what the passenger meant by, "doll dizzy."

Pete walks towards the guy as if to study the moves of a regular Casanova and tries to listen in. One of the surfers taps his buddy, the one who was driving, and points our way.

"Hey, boys, gonna catch the show?" says the driver.

"Oh. Umm, yeah, but, we don't have any money." I tell him.

Of course this is a lie. Well, only kind of. Our money was useless here. I mean, sure the presidents were the same and they had the same basic design, but I wasn't willing to take that chance.

"That's okay. I think I can cover you," the driver says while thumbing through his wallet.

"Really?" I ask in disbelief.

"Sure! A coupla kids out on the town with no money. What else are ya gonna do?"

Dr Jekyll and Mr. Hyde . . . I can only imagine what kind of low budget, black and white horror movie we are in for. It's probably one of those movies they show on the Classics channel. Oh well, I don't know what else we can do to occupy our time. We need to take our minds off of tomorrow.

I thank the surfer stranger as we all approach

87

the ticket counter. His friend is still chatting it up with the girl at the phone booth, who is waiting for her girlfriend to finish up.

"Come on, Sid! Quit flapping your lips," shouts the driver to his hypnotized friend. "Look at him, wouldya? He thinks he's a cool cat, but he needs to hit the silk because that doll is going steady with a G.I."

Next time we time travel, I need a slang translation dictionary. At least I get the gist of what he is trying to tell me. All we need right now is an angry, jealous soldier stopping by.

The flirtatious guy, Sid, looks up at the girl in a manner which suggests, "Is this true?" The girl nods in the affirmative and that's that. Pete and the broken-hearted Hawaiian rejoin us in line.

"I'm Chuck," says the altruistic driver. "And the doll chaser is Sid. Those there are Harry and Benny," he says pointing to the other two surfers.

" He's Pete and I'm Jon," I respond in kind.

"Nice to meet you," says Chuck as we move up in line. "Hey, Pete, you've got a good eye for cars, bud!"

"Ha, yeah thanks, Chuck. My dad builds all sorts of model kits and he especially likes the classics, err, um, I mean, one day I'm sure that Woody will be a classic, ya know what I mean? Right, Jon?"

"Yeah, sure," I say as I roll my eyes.

"So are you two on vacation on this beautiful

island of ours?" asks Chuck.

"Yup, sure are," says Pete.

"That's killer diller! Your mom and dad must be pretty swell letting you go out alone like this. My old man woulda flipped his wig!" comments Chuck.

"Ha ha, yup. They are pretty swell I guess." Pete giggles as I do my best to emulate forties slang.

We approach the box office where Chuck and the locals graciously pay for us. I have no idea why. All we did was compliment his car. I am not complaining, however, and I know Pete feels the same. I only hope they are so kind when we reach the concessions stand. Time travel must make you hungry 'cuz I'm starving.

"Here you go, boys." Chuck hands us our tickets as we continue to process in the line full of anxious movie-goers.

"Glad we got here when we did. Take a look," Harry says. We take a look behind us and see that the ticket line goes down the block and around the next corner.

"I can't wait to see Lana Turner," says Sid, the doll dizzy one. "She is some kinda dame. Ingrid Bergman, too," he says while starring at the promotional movie poster that features a small picture of Bergman on the bottom.

We walk inside the theatre and hand our tickets to the ticket taker. She is standing in front of this tall, red, wooden podium where she rips the ticket in half and drops the remainder down a slot on

89

top. The group of us process towards our movie, passing the concession stand. I glance over and smell the rich, warm, buttery popcorn being freshly popped in an old-fashioned hot air popper. I pause and Pete bumps into me. Chuck laughs and asks if we want something. Score one for the future guys! We get some food then catch up with the rest of the moviegoers.

My tub of popcorn is almost gone and we haven't even taken our seats yet. Next is the hot dog. Probably the most unregulated, unhealthy hotdog I've ever had, but man does it taste soooo good.

We walk into the auditorium and take the seats in the center row. Pete sits to my left and, luckily for me, the seat to my right is empty. I can stretch out a bit. I remove the time device from my back pocket and tuck it between my legs. This way I won't crush it and can keep my eye on it.

I rotate it so the flashing light is unseen. We settle into our seats, the lights go down and a news reel starts to run . . . "Hitler's war machine is halted outside Moscow by the fierce Russian winter and die-hard Soviet troops . . ." The story continues with footage, the allied response and other information pertaining to the war in Europe. I guess Japan is out of the news spotlight for a bit. I don't know how it's possible, but with us being in Hawaii on the eve of the attack, I honestly forgot about the Nazis and the Atlantic theatre altogether. The importance of this time period is just immeasurable. I snap out of it, regain my focus and watch the movie as it begins.

CHAPTER NINE

"I'm Dr. Jekyll! I'm Dr. Henry Jeckyll, I'm Dr. Henry Jeckyll," exclaims Spencer Tracy from the illuminated screen. We are a good ways into the movie and I have to admit, although I am jaded by modern special effects, and this flick is in black and white, it is pretty good. If they remade it today, I am sure the color would be nice, but I know there would be unnecessary aspects that would detract from the total message of the Robert Louis Stevenson masterpiece. Although, it would be pretty cool. I bet they are making a new one right now, back in our time that is.

It's nice to relax and just enjoy the moment of the movie. But wait. I spoke to soon. Although it's turned over so it can't be seen, the green light has just increased in intensity and brightness. I try to cover it some more but it's just no use. It's like a light house in the pitch black that is the movie theatre.

"Jon, what are you doing?" whispers Pete.

"The light is acting up again and it's super

bright."

"Yeah, tell me about it. Come on! They're gonna kick us out and make us show it to them or something!"

"Well, what should we do?"

I don't have any idea of what to do with it. But we gotta do something, and fast. I look around and spot the outline of a side door. It's not an official exit. There are no signs so it must be some sort of delivery door or something. It's our nearest and quickest escape. Sorry, Mr. Hyde, we gotta bail!

"Pete, come on, let's go."

"Yeah, yeah, shut it off," Pete mutters without taking his eyes off the screen. He was now fully entranced by the movie. I reach over and pull him towards me spilling his handful of popcorn all over his lap. "We have to go!"

He gets up and we head to the service door at the bottom of the theatre. I try to push it open but it doesn't budge. I give it a good shove with my shoulder and it creaks a little bit. "Hey, knock it off down there," a voice calls from the crowd. One more push and the door finally opens.

We walk through the doorway and end up in a side alley. It's your typical creepy alley. It has more of big-city, dirty alley feeling than a simple alley in Honolulu. There are over flowing trash cans and dumpsters and discarded wooden pallets, stacked next to the rear door of what appears to be a seafood restaurant. The device's light is intense. It glows an eerie green and brightens up the poorly lit alley like a Halloween glow stick.

Once again, I shove it in my back pocket as we head back towards the front of the building near the main street. Our walk is halted as a black sedan pulls up at the end of the alley. I think nothing of it, but the driver seems to be staring right at us. We keep our cool, regain composure and continue to walk towards the main street. There seems to be two other people in the car, one in the passenger seat and one in the back.

I keep my eyes on the driver and, there is just something off about him, something . . . I can't place it but . . .

"Dude, is that Jackson?" Pete asks in disbelief. That's it. He's right. It was Jackson. I don't know how, but he found us. He came back in time and found us in 1941 Oahu.

Jackson realizes we recognize him. He shoots us that same evil grin as he did from the ice cream truck. We start back pedaling, heading back towards the theatre door. Jackson opens his door and exits the car as does his passenger. And wow, wouldn't you know it? It's the "lady in red." This is crazy. I just can't believe they found us. I mean, who are these people? The last time we encountered them we had a gun drawn on us. I don't even want to think what will happen this time.

The light on the device is brightly shining through my pocket. We reach the door and I pull to open it, but nothing. It's locked. No matter how hard I pull it, it won't budge. Of course, this being a stereotypical, creepy alley, there is a dead end about ten feet away from us. I go across the alley to the wooden pallets and try the door. No luck. It's locked as well.

Jackson and the woman walk closer and closer as the device's light gets brighter and brighter. She is holding some other electronic device that has a similar light and a beeping that sort of mimics the pulsing of our green light. Of course! It must be a homing device or something! How else could they have found us? This thing must have a GPS or something built into it. Just our luck!

"Surprised to see us, boys?" Jackson shouts down the alley as they approach us. Pete frantically bangs on the huge iron door of the theatre, screaming, "Let us in! Let us in!"

"Ha ha. Well, well, well. It is nice to meet you boys," says the woman. "Let me introduce mys . . . "

Just then the door flies open. It's Chuck! He takes one look at the scared expressions on our faces and peers down the alley towards the two quickly approaching silhouettes. Chuck grabs my collar, yells, "Come on," and pulls me back into the theatre. Pete is on my heels and without hesitation, pushes us in. Chuck does not wait for the door to shut on its own spring-hinge power and forces it to close. Jackson and the lady's footsteps can be heard

95

stomping down the back alley. Pete gives it a final push to ensure it is locked on the outside. We have to act fast. It'll only take a minute for them to come into the theatre.

"Enough with the noise!" an angry man shouts from the back balcony. The light on the device is as bright as ever and we're back in the quiet, ultra dark auditorium.

"Chuck! Hey, Chuck, sit down, man. Get back here," one of Chuck's friends says in a shouting sort of whisper. Chuck waves him off as we head to the front of the theatre. He pulls us aside in a corner.

"Okay, What's going on, fellas?"

"Long story short," Pete says, "those are bad guys and they are after us."

"Great. What are you guys up to?" Chuck inquires. "Never mind! Follow me! I parked around back."

As if he has done this before, Chuck leads us to an entryway behind the movie screen. We creep behind the screen as it is projected on the other side. There, 'Dr. Jekyll' has just finished transforming into 'Mr. Hyde.' Some transformation. Honestly, right now I would rather change into 'Mr. Hyde' instead of attempting to tackle the transformation from a twenty-first century kid to a kid from the 1940's. We can relate in another way as well; Mr. Hyde . . . is being chased.

Chuck continues in the dark, avoiding wires, cables and a huge wooden ladder. We finally reach the back exit of the entire theatre. The Woody is parked there and is looking better than ever. We race to the car as Chuck tells us to get in. He starts the engine, and waits for Pete and me to open the massive back door.

This thing is built like a tank. Now I know what our neighbor, old man Jack, was talking about. He was referring to an old Ford advertisement he was selling at a yard sale when he said, "They don't make 'em like they used to!"

We finally throw the door open and jump in the back bench seat. Chuck puts it in first gear and we tear off.

"Hey, Stop! Stop!" I turn to find Jackson behind us, waving his hands and yelling. It's kinda weird. It's as if he assumes we would really stop for him. Is he crazy?

Chuck drives and slows down as we turn onto the main street. We pass the theatre entrance and, once again, see the black sedan. The sketchy boss lady is standing up against the far side of the car, her back towards us. As we pass the car from behind I see the other figure in the backseat moving around.

"Slow down, Chuck!" I demand, as we pass by the car. I examine the back seat of the car expecting to see one of the earlier cronies from the plantation house, most likely Leo, the stubby one. But I am wrong. Staring right into my eyes is Abby. Those bastards got her!

CHAPTER TEN

We continue to drive out of the downtown area towards Diamond Head, a famous, dormant volcano on the southeastern coast of Oahu. Pete leans over and points it out. He unenthusiastically mentions that he hiked it last year. We are both still in shock; not only did these creepers somehow come back in time to find us, but they also have Abby held captive.

Chuck pulls over near an old pier and parks the car. We are safe now. Or, at least I hope we are. Chuck turns around, looks square at us and says, "Okay, fellas, now listen hear. Ya hafta tell me what's going on so I know what I'm involved in. That guy was givin' me the heebie jeebies, and good!"

Chuck is scared and it shows. Well, we are all scared. But at least Pete and I know the reason as to why. Chuck scans us up and down several times before saying," Come on, fellas, out with it!"

I look at Pete and he looks back. We just sit, speechless, without a clue in the world of what we should or shouldn't say. I mean, we have got to tell him something. He *is* involved now. And as much as I didn't want to affect the past, here is another example of how we have. Chuck never did this in 1941. He never met us nor did he buy us movie tickets. He never saved our asses in that alleyway either. But the thing is . . . now, he did. We owed it to him to tell him, at least a little.

I open my door and get out. You basically have to crawl out of this thing. The back seat is about as long as my couch in my living room! No wonder why back seats of old cars were so popular, back in the day.

Pete exits and Chuck shortly follows. The three of us walk toward the hood of the Woody and lean on it. With a huge inhale and a giant sigh, I let out an, "Okay. Here's what we can tell you." Upon hearing those words, Pete's eyebrows rise to compliment the scowl on his face.

"It's ok Pete, were in deep now." We have to.

"But, you just told me . . ." Pete rubs his temples as if he has a headache, "That is the exact opposite of what you just told me, Jon!?"

"Pete, you trusted me before at the plantation house. You trust me now too, right?"
Pete exhales with a, "Yes, of course I do, Jon."

Pete slides his body down the wagon until he plops to the ground and sits Indian style on mixture of sand and gravel.

"Well," I say as I ponder where to start. "That guy and that lady back there at the theatre, well, we kinda have something of theirs."

"You two hoisted something from them?" Chuck asks in disbelief with a giant grin on his face. "Golly guys, this is just swell! I didn't expect you two to be the criminal type."

"No, no," I insist, "It's nothing like that. I mean, we found something of theirs and we had to use it"

"A gun! Oh, please tell me you did not have to use a gun!"

"No, ha ha, it was . . ." Pete looks up at me, knowing that this guy won't believe what he's about to hear.

I continue with, "It was this." I pull the device out of my pocket and display it with both hands, keeping a firm grip on it. I still can't be too sure who to trust. Chuck looks at it and says, "Oh, that crazy flashlight that you guys had in the theatre? Those goons are chasing you just for that thing?"

This will definitely get him. "It's not a flashlight. It's, well, a little more complicated than that."

"Ok. So it's a *fancy* flashlight, ha ha. It does have all the bells and whistles: lights, all those buttons, fancy display and a, well, a trigger?"

"Yeah, but, Chuck, it's still not a flashlight. It's, It's . . ." I shuffle my feet in the sand.

"It's a time machine, man!" shouts Pete.

"Wha?" mutters a very baffled Chuck. Pete continues, "They lost it, we found it. They chased us so we hit the button and came back here to 1940 and . . ."

"1941," says Chuck.

"Huh?" asks Pete.

"It's 1941, not 1940."

"Ok, forty, forty-one, same to me. It's old back here, dude. Anyway, they somehow came back and tracked us down and now they have our friend, Abby. There. I said it. That's it. Sorry, Jon, but he had to hear it."

"I know, Pete, it's ok," I say punch-tapping him on the shoulder.

"Just a little more subtle manner would have been nice!"

We both stand in silence and wait for Chuck's reply. He looks baffled and bewildered beyond belief, as was expected. I mean, we're from over 70 years in the future and it still amazes *me* that we traveled through time. But seeing is believing.

Chuck backs up, smiles and says, "Good one, Pete." He forces a chuckle. "Now I'm serious, those two meant business, so tell me the truth."

"That is the truth, Chuck."

"What? Are you . . . are you serious? Whoa! Fellas, this is like Jules Verne stuff.
This . . . this is madness!" Chuck says with his hand on his forehead.

"This is Sparta!!" shouts Pete followed by an awkward laugh.

"Really, Pete? Really?" I say shaking my
101

head.

"Sorry, Jon."

Chuck shakes his head and says, "So you guys are serious? No foolin?

"No foolin," Pete and I both say. Chuck leans back on the hood of his Woody.

"This is amazing. I mean, I knew you two were kind of screwy but I just couldn't put my finger on it."

"Hey!" Pete interrupts, "What do you mean, screwy?"

"Ha ha, no offense boys. But you two don't seem like your average tourists or out-of-towners, ya know?"

"I can finally take off these stupid socks!" says Pete.

"Well, we are tourists," I say, "But not only from a different place, but a different time altogether.

"Gee whiz! You guys have to tell me 'bout stuff! What's it like? Flying cars? Robot maids and all that jazz?"

Chuck was digging things alright. It's kinda hard to believe how easy it was to convince him. But I mean, who knows? Everyone is different, right? Here I am, the time traveler, and still can't believe it myself.

Chuck leans in like a little child hearing about Santa for the first time. He is fully strapped into a roller coaster ride of the brain. It weaves you in and out of fascinating, yet unpractical and unreasonable visions of the future.

Just like my dad used to say, "Why aren't we living in the Jetsons' Age yet? Where are our flying cars and robot maids?" It's as if the world will never reach what is termed "the future" unless those two inventions are realized. I don't even know what Dad was talking about. I think he told me it was an old cartoon he used to watch when he was growing up. I never caught any episodes of it on the cartoon channel. I will have to catch some episodes online, when we return home, that is. Because right now, there is no "online" yet, let alone anything that resembles a flying car.

"Well? Robot maids?" Asks Chuck. I snap out of it and reply with, "No, no. It's nothing like that. I mean, there are some pretty amazing advancements but no flying cars yet.

"Wow! Like what?" he asks.

"All sorts of stuff: DVDs, portable tablets, cars that park themselves, the world wide web, and we have even . . ."

"Geez a web as big as the world? What does it do?" Chuck wanted a lesson in Future 101.

" We've been to the moon!" I reply.

"The moon! Now I know you're foolin, right? No? Ok. Wow! The moon? What about world events? They are having this huge conflict overseas right now. It's an all European and Asian war and some people are already calling it the Second World War. You guys have gotta let me know what happens with this one. Do we stay out of it completely or do we get into the heat of things like the Great War? I gotta know, please, man.

"Uh, Chuck," I stutter, "listing a few new inventions is one thing, but telling you what happens with future events is totally another.

"You know, don't you? Please, you have got to tell me what happens. My dad is in the service. I just need to know what's gonna happen!"

"What branch?" asks Pete.

"Coast Guard," says Chuck.

"And he is out to sea right now?"

"No. He's at headquarters, right near Pearl. Why? Why, Jon? Tell me!" Chuck grabs my collar again but unlike the rescue from the alley, he didn't do this out of the kindness of his heart for my safety. He was angry. This was out of fear and concern for his father.

I can totally understand where he is coming from. Oh, and did I mention his other arm is raised with a giant fist at the end, aiming square at my face?

"HEY!" shouts Pete. Chuck draws back his fist and lays off.

"Sorry. I'm so sorry guys. I just . . . if anything happens, I just . . ." Chuck lets me go and backs away.

"It's ok, Chuck," I insist," I mean, of course we know stuff, I mean, but you can understand my hesitation and our dilemma. If we tell you what ha . . ."

"I know, I know, "Chuck interjects with a frustrated tone. "If you tell me one thing, that affects another and that affects another, and so on and so forth. I have read science fiction books."

"That's exactly right, Chuck. I'm glad you understand why we. . ."

"I'm glad YOU understand," Chuck interjects, "that you need to tell me. I would do the same for you."

"Just tell him, Jon. Come on, what more can go wrong?" Pete opines.

I take a deep breath and reluctantly reply, "I guess."

Dare I ask myself what more could go wrong? All the "what if" scenarios run through my head. What if we tell Chuck and he tells his father and then we attack Japan before they attack us or we are never attacked or . . . just the thought of all the variables gives me a migraine. When we get back to our time, let's be honest, *if* we get back to our time, the real time, what if it's all different because of what has happened? Then again, there is obviously more than one time machine out there if those two got back here somehow. Who's to say the past isn't changing all the time, all around us? I just don't know anymore. Too bad there is no time traveling handbook or something.

"Ok, Chuck, you ready for this?"

"As ready as I'll ever be, I guess," he says.

"Ok, so something happens tomorrow."

105

"Tomorrow? That fast?" What is it? Do we join the war and attack the Germans?

"Um, not exactly," says Pete.

The light on the device starts blinking heavily once again. Last time this happened our pursuers were only a few yards away.

"Look!" cries Pete.

"I know! I know!"

"Get in the car, boys." Chuck commands as he opens the driver's side door.

CHAPTER ELEVEN

The green light on the device matches the eerie, golden glow of headlights as they round the corner. The black sedan makes its appearance and slows to a crawl, coming up behind us and blinding us with its high beams. There is no doubt it's Jackson and the lady and, I pray, Abby.

"Let's go, boys!" Chuck screams as he hops in the car.

"We can't! They have our friend. We can't keep running. We need to get her back!" I command.

The car comes to a stop. It idles about twenty yards away. Chuck steps back out of the Woody and slams the door. We stand here, blinded by the headlights until they are finally shut off. A figure steps out of the car. Our eyes are still adjusting and I can't quite make out who it is . . . "Abby!" I cry. Pete starts to run towards her, but Chuck and I reach out and stop him.

She is gagged, hands behind her back, presumably tied. Other than that, she looks ok. Well, as ok as she could be.

The passenger's side door opens and out

steps the lady. She repositions Abby in front of her and holds her close. She looks pissed. And I guess she should be.

"Ok. So we were interrupted before. My name is Klara Beich. As you can see, we have your little friend," the lady says with an accent that I have never heard from her. I just can't place it right now but she definitely sounds a lot different than before.

"Now, this is how we do this. We make a simple, easy, little trade. We are sorry that we had to drag her all the way back here to the 1940's, but since you decided to activate the temporal, we had no other choice.

"Yeah, well we had no choice but to pull the trigger, you crazy bitch! Jackson was about to shoot us!" exclaims Pete.

"No, no, Jackson is a puppy dog. His bark is bigger than his bite."

"Oh, yeah. I'm sure you are all innocent, what with your covert ice cream truck and trunk full of decals and advertising signs," I say.

"So you have done your homework, little one? Here is what's going to happen. We trade you the girl and you give us the device."

"Why do you want it so much? You obviously have another one if you traveled back in time to find us."

"You would think so wouldn't you? "But, you see, they work together." She holds up another time device. "This one works with the other one. One is primary and one is secondary. You see, you took the primary one. That is the more important of the two."

"Hold on! We found it! We didn't take anything, lady!" Pete screams.

"Semantics my friend. Either way, all we have is the secondary one. The secondary one is useless without the primary one, so we need them both!

"So, what is the point of the secondary one?" I inquire.

"If you must know, little one, the second one is in case the first travelers have any trouble. A secondary team can come back and assist them.

"So that's how you tracked us down! That green light was some sort of a beacon or GPS, right?

"Yes, you are very bright. It is quite ingenious, actually. Although, I can't take credit for it. It is my grandfather's blueprint." She pauses.

Believe it or not she looks as if she is holding back a tear. She starts speaking again, "Look I have no time for this chit chat. The clock is ticking. We need to . . ."

"You need to what? Why *this* date, after all? Why now? Why the night before the seventh? Just exactly what are you planning? I try my best to force an answer from her.

"Hmmm, not only bright but full of knowledge about your history lessons too, hmmm?"

Just then another car pulls up: a police car.

109

Its lights flash on and off twice as it pulls in behind the sedan. The woman, Klara, quickly shoves Abby into the back seat of the car, right before the cop turns on his giant flood light. We hear him radio dispatch to inform them of his location. He gets out of the squad car, takes his flashlight from his belt and approaches us.

"Evening," he says.

"Good evening, officer," speaks the lady, but this time with her American accent.

"This your automobile?" he asks, pointing to her car. Jackson, still in the front seat, is leaning towards the back, gun in hand. He undoubtedly is ready to act as he holds the gun towards Abby.

"Yes, sir. Yes it is. Well, my husband's that is to say."

"You three," he says, looking past the Klara and back to us. "Are you with these two?"

"No, sir," Chuck answers. "We had a flat, uh, but it's fixed now. We'll be heading out."

"Alright then, boys, carry on," he says as he points down the road with his flashlight.

"Young lady, you two were going mighty fast around the bend back there. I clocked you at forty- seven miles per hour." He approaches Klara on the right side of the car. Jackson faces forward and lowers his gun but I am sure it is still aimed towards Abby.

"Hey! You, in the driver's seat. Slowly step out," says the policeman.

110

"Look, officer, we're sorry. We were just lost and trying to find our hotel. It's been a long flight and perhaps you can help us." Klara is trying her best to get rid of the cop. Jackson slowly steps out of the car. His gun is nowhere to be seen.

"Come on guys," says Chuck. We all reluctantly get back into the Woody. Chuck starts her up and makes a slow u-turn in the gravel heading back in the direction of the others.

"Step over here, sir," I hear the cop demand as we drive at a creep pace towards them. Jackson walks to the trunk of the car and quickly reaches inside his pocket.

"Hold it right there!" The cop commands while drawing his side arm and aiming it square at Jackson's head. At this, Chuck also stops the Woody.

"Whoa, now, officer, it's just a smoke. Just a smoke, that's all." Jackson continues around to the rear of the car. The cop keeps his gun aimed at Jackson's face. Jackson pulls out a cigarette box and presents it to the officer "See, sir? That's all." The officer looks satisfied and slowly holsters his gun.

Jackson continues to present the cigarette box to the cop, even though the officer seems to believe him. He squeezes the box and a thin stream of orange liquid shoots out at the officer. It lands on him and immediately starts to eat through his shirt. It even appears to be burning through a small portion of his badge.

The cop looks down at his burning chest and

badge. "You, son of a bitch!" he yells as he drops his flashlight. He redraws his gun and opens fire. The first bullet strikes Jackson square in the shoulder. The officer runs back to his car, and tears off his shirt as fast as he is able. Jackson puts his hand on his struck shoulder and cringes in pain. He reaches through the open door and grabs his gun and begins to return fire. The cop seeks shelter in his car and gets on the radio. He calls for back up while firing several more rounds.

"You, idiot!" cries Klara as she runs toward the shore and away from the gunfire.

Chuck drives us closer to the sedan and stops behind it, dodging the barrage of bullets. He opens his door.

"Chuck, what are you doing, man!?" cries Pete. Chuck crawls out of the car, ducks down and hides between the Woody and the sedan. He grabs for the sedan's rear door handle and finds Abby lying on the floor.

The officer and Jackson continue the gunfight. The cop shines the flood light right into Jackson's eyes, blinding him from his target.

Chuck reaches inside and pulls Abby out. I hop into the driver's seat, knowing full well that we don't have a second to waste. Chuck throws Abby into the back seat of the Woody, while Pete pulls her in. She is still tied up and gagged. Pete gives her a final tug and pulls her all the way in. Without closing the door Chuck says, "Go, Go, Go!!!" and jumps in.

I assume the role of driver and grasp the enormous steering wheel. It's as big as a garbage can lid. I slam on the gas and we peel out, almost hitting two other cars on their way up the mountain. The sedan and police car get smaller and smaller and finally disappear in the rearview mirror.

I speed all the way around the base of Diamond Head on the opposite side and head back to the busy streets of downtown Honolulu. We pull over onto a side street near an active nightclub and park the car.

CHAPTER TWELVE

Chuck is just finishing untying and un-gagging Abby. They really did quite a job on her.

"Thank you. Thank you so much," Abby says while trying to catch her breath. "Do you guys have any water?"

"You mean those bastards didn't even give you water?" asks Pete in disbelief.

"Here," Chuck says, as he rummages around in the back of his wagon and pulls out a dusty mug. Pete takes it, exits the car and walks over to the side of the building where a garden hose is wound up on the ground. He unravels it a bit, turns on the spigot, sprays the mug clean and then fills it with water.

"Abby, thank God you're ok," I say as Pete hands me the mug through the car window. Abby grabs the water and drinks it as if it was the most delicious drink ever made.

"Jon . . . Jon . . . they . . . those two, Jackson and Klara, they . . .

"They are up to no good I'll bet," says Pete.

"Wow, Sherlock, ya think? They kidnapped

114

your friend and shot at a cop. They aren't headed to sainthood, that's for sure.

"Shut up, Chuck! You know what I meant!" said Pete as Chuck smiles a goofy grin.

"You guys, listen!" Abby takes another gulp of water. "I overheard them talking . . ."

She is struggling. "Abby, just rest a bit, ok? Take your time and start from the beginning. I'm Chuck, by the way."

"Thanks so much, Chuck. Nice to meet you."

"Ha, likewise, I'm sure, but we can get past all those formalities for the time being. Those clowns still have the ability to track us down and who knows how long the cops can hold them off?

"Ok, so after you guys vanished, I mean . . . you just straight up disappeared. I screamed, like an idiot." She grabs one last gulp of water until the mug runs dry.

"Yeah, I bet that must have been pretty epic to see us disappear, huh?" asks Pete. Were we all glowing and shiny and oh, was there like a big boom of energy when we left?"

"No." Abby says, "Nothing like that at all. You just, you just weren't there anymore."

"Oh, ok. It was totally different for us."

"Believe me, I know," says Abby. I took the same route you did, don't forget!"

"Very true!" says Pete.

"Ok, now, get back to the story. What happened?" asks Chuck, getting impatient.

"So, they were able to catch up to me. I mean, I could have beaten them easily in a foot race but I was just so astonished and amazed at what I'd just seen. I was so worried about you guys." Her lower lip starts to quiver. Pete, now back in the car, leans over and gives her a giant hug.

"Thanks, Pete. They took me back to their, well, their *hideout*; I guess you would call it. It's that abandoned warehouse over on Third, close to the comic shop. You should have seen this place. It was full of schematics and maps and photos and all sorts of boards full of information.

"Information on what?" Chuck inquires. "Just what are these guys up to?"

Abby continues, "Information on Pearl Harbor. Um, Jon, I'm no geography wiz or anything, but what with all the palm trees and I am pretty sure that was Diamond Head back there . . . I am guessing we're in Hawaii, huh?

"Yup, sure are." I confirm. "Not a geography wiz my a . . ."

"What?"

"Nothing. Nothing. I was just saying we're on Oahu, ha ha." I say as I give her a wink.

"That figures." Abby says.

"Wait, what? What are they planning? Jon, I knew you knew something!" Chuck exclaims. Now I have no choice but to tell him.

"I was about to tell you, but then they showed up and all this happened. Just chill and I'll

116

explain now."

"Chill, what do you mean, it's like 90 degrees out here?"

"It means to just relax and calm down. Ok?" I explain.

Abby looks at Chuck and smiles, just now realizing that there is somewhat of a language barrier, or at least a *slang* barrier between us.

"Jon, they had info on Pearl Harbor and the attack. The bulk of the info was on the route of the approaching fleet and the location of their six carriers and coordinates, and all this stuff, guys!"

Chuck now has a scowl on his face and shakes his head from side to side.

"Attack!!! That crazy dame and wisenheimer are gonna attack the Pearl, all alone? You guys, please! You are killing me here! Fill me in already!"

Chuck is right. He has waited patiently, for the most part anyways. It's time to fill him in.

I look back at Abby and Pete. They both nod. I turn around and face Chuck, take a deep breath and exhale.

"Ok, Chuck, you ready for this?" I ask.

"Yes! Yes! Please!"

"America does enter the war, that is to say, World War II. It is prompted by a surprise attack on Pearl Harbor, on Sunday morning, December 7, 1941."

"The Krauts attack us? Tomorrow?!?"

"No," says Abby, "not Germany, Chuck,

117

Japan."

"Yeah," I continue, "The Japanese will attack tomorrow morning. They have been planning it for months.

"For months?" Chuck looks up towards the sky, his breathing quickens. "But, they have representatives and diplomats in Washington, right now, trying to work things out."

"This is true," I add, "but the diplomats' deadline on the oil embargo being lifted, has passed. And Japan needs oil to make war."

"Trust us, Chuck," adds Pete leaning out the window, "They attack in the morning. Sorry, dude."

"Well, how do we fair? I mean, we win, right?" asks Chuck.

"Overall, yes, but it will be a long and grueling war against the Axis powers: Tojo's Imperial Japan, Hitler's Nazi Germany and Mussolini's Fascist Italy. Tomorrow, however, is a total shock. I mean, our government recognized the potential threat of a Japanese attack, but never really thought it could happen to us directly. We figured it would be somewhere else in the Pacific.

Chuck, still looking as if he has seen a ghost asks, "So we fight all three of them?"

"Yes," I reply, "We fight in both the Atlantic and Pacific theatres."

"Theatre? What do you mean, theatre?" Chuck inquires.

"I got this one, Chuck!" Pete happily says,

118

with a huge grin on his face. I nod my head and laugh.

"Well, World War II is divided up into two campaigns, referred to as theatres: The Pacific, where we fight against Japan and the Atlantic, where we fight against Hitler and Mussolini. Right, Jon?" he asks seeking approval.

"Oh, my God!" Chuck cries.

This is, of course, a shock for Chuck and not an occasion for playing trivia. This is *his* time, *his* place, *his* life and *his* world. To hold this knowledge is incredible. It's knowing the outcome of the most famous war the world has ever, and hopefully, *will* ever know.

"I just can't believe this. I mean." Chuck looks down at the ground then back up at the sky. His eyes are aimlessly searching for something, perhaps answers, that will not come.

"I mean, I do believe you guys, but I just . . . so what actually happens, tomorrow, I mean?

"Tell him, Jon," insists Abby.

"All right. So the Japanese have six carriers, steaming our way right now." I still don't believe it when I hear myself speak the words explaining it to Chuck. I can't believe that we are standing so close to history.

"They will have two waves of attack. They were originally considering three, but the guy in charge, Admiral Yamamoto, will realize he will lose the element of surprise and will cancel the last wave. They will hit our airfields simultaneously: Kaneohe, Hickam, Ewa, Bellows and Wheeler, to wipe out any potential air to air combat threat. The Japanese will do a great job at destroying hundreds of our planes and we will only get a handful off the ground. The second wave will finish things up. They will drop torpedoes and dumb bombs and devastate our entire Pacific Fleet."

Chuck shakes his head back and forth. He has an expression of belief and disbelief all in one.

"Wait. Torpedoes? From planes? But . . . they would sink to the bottom! The harbor is too shallow," Chuck maintains.

"That's true, but they came up with a solution. They made this little wooden box, like a fin, and placed it around the propellers of the torpedoes, which keeps them afloat.

"Those Jap bastards thought of everything," Chuck says with an upturned, snarl lip.

"Well, yeah, but it's funny because they're not, um . . . 'Jap bastards' anymore. We are really close allies now after the bomb and our rebuilding of Japan."

"Rebuilding!? What? And what bomb? I hope you mean tons and tons of bombs?"

"Well, that's another story all together." Pete laughs a great laugh and Abby smiles.

"So, Jon, this attack obviously brings us into war right? How soon?"

120

"The next day. President Roosevelt calls it 'a date which will live in infamy.' It's the last time Congress will declare war, but def not the last time US troops see combat."

"Jon . . . Jon . . . how many dead?"

"Tomorrow, and tomorrow alone, with the complete sinking of four of our battleships, almost 3,000. It will be the biggest attack on American soil for around 50 years.

"Oh, yeah," says Pete, "last year we went to see the Arizona memorial in the harbor."

"The Arizona? The USS Arizona?" Chuck questions.

"Yeah, a lot of sailors went down with it," I reply.

"You mean, *will* go down with it. They are not gone yet."

"Yeah, sorry Chuck," I apologize.

"So, we lose our whole Pacific Fleet?"

"Well, the good news, if we can call any of this good news, is that we don't lose our seven Pacific-stationed carriers.

"Why not? Who warns them? Why are they so lucky?" Chuck asks.

"I dunno, Chuck, they are just all out doing other things. It's a blessing really. We couldn't have won the war without them. The carriers prove to be a crucial part of the war in the Pacific Theatre."

"Ohhhhh, Jon, tell 'em about the mini subs!" Pete interrupts.

"Yeah, but they were pretty useless," Abby adds.

"Yeah, but, I mean, they are still pretty cool, ya know? I mean, although they sucked and epically failed at life," says Pete.

"True. It sucks that it took forever to relay the message that we spotted a mini sub before the air assault even started." I reply.

Chuck leans back and takes it all in. I can only imagine what he's thinking. Thinking that the world is turned upside down, feeling helpless and not knowing what could be done or, moreover, what *should* be done.

He kicks the gravel towards a group of passing naval officers exiting the nightclub. The gravel rolls and smacks against the side of an officers neatly kept dress shoes. He stops and looks towards Chuck, who quickly apologizes. Seeing the men in uniform just reminds Chuck of one thing: his father.

"I hafta tell my father. I just hafta! You guys understand, right?"

"Well, even if we didn't agree with it, because of the possibility of changing how life is supposed to play out, we definitely understand," I tell him.

"True and we wouldn't begin to know how to stop you!" Pete insists, "You're a giant compared to us!"

The light on the device begins to flash faster and faster, as before. That could only mean one thing;

they were getting close to us again. Klara made it quite clear that they needed this primary device to go anywhere. The other one was basically obsolete without its partner. I am pretty sure Klara and Jackson will stop at nothing to get it back from us, a couple of kids, trapped in the past before one of the greatest surprise attacks ever.

"You guys. What are we gonna do?" I ask, out of options.

"Quick!" yells Chuck, "Get in the wagon!"

The light continues pulsing faster and faster, almost becoming solid. Out of nowhere, the black sedan speeds down the main drag and comes to an abrupt stop right in front of us. They have tracked us once again.

Jackson grins his evil grin as we are all caught off guard, once again scrambling to get back into the car. But this time, instead of getting out and chasing us, Klara waves Jackson on and motions for him to continue to drive towards the main road out of town. The car speeds off as quickly as it stopped.

"What the? Why did they keep going?" Abby asks. "I mean, I was their last bargaining chip so obviously they don't have that anymore but, like, they still need the main time machine thing to get out of here right?"

"That's the way I understood it," I agree. "There must be something more important on their minds right now. And I bet it has something to do with what you saw back at their hideout. Abby, you gotta tell us what you saw there. As much as you can remember!"

"Well yeah, I mean, like I said, they had all these photos and charts and maps and things. And most of them, instead of focusing on Pearl itself, were surprisingly focused on the Japanese fleet and, and . . . oh yeah, there was even this book called umm, IDK but it's like, all about the surprise of the Japanese. But the strangest one of all was this one map. It had these red arrows drawn from Pearl Harbor, well not Pearl Harbor, but definitely from the same island, off to the coast, and like, I would say, from the North West of Oahu. The arrows were headed toward a big circle surrounding six little magnet cut outs of Japanese flags." Abby describes.

"What do you think that means, Jon?" asks Pete.

"It means . . . it means they wanna do what we all want to do, but know we can't." I say, shocked.

"Whoa, whoa, whoa, Jon!" says Pete.

"I know, Pete, I know."

"So. You're tellin' me that those two, those criminals, those bums who kidnapped your friend, and shot at us, want to help prevent Pearl Harbor from ever being attacked?" Chuck asks.

"Yes, Chuck. I mean, it looks that way, right?"

"Make sense, from what I saw in that room," agrees Abby.

"So, wait, Jon, let me get this straight. Those jerks are actually trying to do something good? That seems so out of character for them.

"I agree, Chuck. But there is obviously more than meets the eye, something disturbing, no doubt.

Two black and white squad cars race down the street, lights and sirens a blazing!
The second car takes the corner too wide and goes up on the curb. Its half moon hubcap springs off the right rear tire and twirls across the pavement. The officer corrects and gets back on the road. The cars continue down the street in the same direction as Klara and Jackson.

"Abby," I look straight into her eyes, "if you saw a map of the island again, would you be able to pinpoint their starting location? Ya know? Where you said the arrows came from? The Northwest area?"

"Sure, dude, I mean, I am pretty sure I could. Why? What're you thinking?

"I'm thinking we have to find out exactly what's goin' on with those clowns. You guys stay here! I'll be right back!"

I exit the car, shut the door and start jogging down the street. Most of the crowds are gone now. The clock on the bank reads a quarter after one. I need to find a map somewhere but all the touristy places have already closed for the evening.

I stop jogging and look around for someplace, anyplace that would have a map. If this was modern day Oahu, I can only imagine that maps and pamphlets exist everywhere on every street corner. The only thing I can find, however, is a map, plastered to the side of a newspaper stand. It will have to do. Time to tell the others.

"You guys! Let's go!"I shout as I sprint back to the others.

"Did you find a map?" they all ask.

"Yes. No, I mean, kinda. There is one but it's glued on the side of that newsstand from earlier, Pete."

"Ok, hop in." says Chuck.

We get back in the wagon, Chuck at the wheel. It actually takes us a bit longer to reach the newsstand by car since one of the streets was one-way traffic only. Chuck pulls to the side as we reach the stand. We exit and gather over at the map.

"Here, Abby. Look. Where was it?" I ask, while pointing to the map.

"Um . . . Ummm . . ."

"Come on, Abb! yells Pete.

"Shut up, man! Gimmee a minute!"

"You said you could spot it! Pete retorts.

"Well, this isn't exactly the same map. And besides, their map didn't have little points-of-interest palm tree icons all over the place!" Abby squints her eyes as if to see the map better. "And it wasn't covered in chewing gum either!" she adds. To her benefit it is pretty dark and difficult to see. There is a street lamp on the corner but a giant palm tree claims dominance, casting its shadow over the entire block.

"Here," she says. "It was right here!" she cries with excitement. Abby points all the way to the top of the map which has a surfboard icon imprinted on it.

"Are you sure, Abby?" I ask.

"Yeah, that's it, right there!" She confirms.

"That's Waialee!" adds Chuck. "That's what they call the North Shore. Wild waves up there, guys."

"Can you take us there?"

"Sure. It will take a bit to get there so we better hit the road now."

"One minute," I say as Chuck heads back to the car. I want to make sure we all get a good look at this map since we can't take it with us.

"Guys, take a mental snapshot of this map, ok?" We stand here trying to memorize every detail in case we need an escape route. This time we will be prepared.

The old fashioned horn of the Woody honks and we head back. I sit up front next to Chuck, while Abby and Pete sit in the back. She still looks pretty beat up. I can actually see her closer now. She has bruises and cuts and scratches. She is taking it all in stride, though. She seems her normal self. But that's how she is; she tends to keep stuff bottled up as if she's one of the guys. It's funny, though, she should know better. When I get emotional, I get emotional. Forget all the macho stuff. I'm only human. If I find the need to cry, I let it go like Niagara Falls!

127

She catches me staring at a huge bruise on her leg. "What?" she asks. I shake my head and smile at her.

She still has her modern clothes on. I guess Klara and Jackson didn't care about Abby's ability to blend in. And why would they? Especially if they kept her locked up or hidden all the time or, or even worse. Maybe they didn't care if she blended in because they were planning on . . . the thought is unbearable. I swear if they try to hurt her again, or any of us for that matter . . . they're gonna get it good.

CHAPTER THIRTEEN

There seems to be only one route out of downtown and that's where we are headed. We start off in the same direction as the cop cars and the black sedan. We still have no clue what Jackson and Klara are up to. Well, that's not true. Abby's quick recall of the map showed us that they want to go towards the approaching Japanese carriers.

Even so, we still have no idea what they are planning. Are they going to join in on the attack with the Japanese? Or was Pete right? Were they actually trying to prevent the attack from ever happening? One thing is for sure; we are about find out.

We exit Honolulu and head north. Chuck says it should take around an hour to get there. I have no clue what we're going to do once we reach the North Shore, besides seeing the giant turtles that live there. I learned about them in Earth science a few weeks before school let out. After all this, it feels more like years ago.

We should really get the authorities involved. I mean, geez, they are already involved, right? The cops are chasing them all over the place. I gotta see how the others will weigh in on this.

"You guys, I know it's crazy, but I think we should tell the police. I mean, tell them what we know. Or, at least tell the army or something!"

"Jon, you're starting to sound like Pete!" butts in Abby. "No offense, Pete. But, what do you mean, Jon? What are we gonna say. 'Hi, Mr. soldier boy. We are from the future and we were being chased by two lunatics but now we're chasing them, but we don't know exactly why. Oh, did I mention that thousands will die tomorrow?'"

"I guess you're right, Abby. But I mean, the cops already know they are chasing someone. They had a whole shootout back there, remember? We can . . . I dunno. I am out of ideas. You got any better ones?"

"Yeah," says Abby. "We keep driving to the spot on the map and see what they are up to. That's our plan and we should stick with it."

The car is completely quiet. We are all exhausted, physically, mentally, any kind of exhaustion there is, believe me we have it. Emotions are high.

We stay quiet for about ten more minutes. We're all in our own worlds, pondering what we should do, what was about to happen and more so, what would happen if we intervened. Would our futures be the same? Would we have a future? What about America's future? What if we can't even make it back to present day? Sure we have each other, sure I love the past, but, I also love my life in the world that I know. I love sitting in the oak and just chillin'. I love the fall when the new school year approaches. I love Christmas morning around the tree with Mom and Dad. What will happen to all of that if we can't get back? I have enough worries about my future without all of these extra possibilities.

"Hey, Chuck," I ask, "You ever wonder about your future?"

"Well, yeah, now more than ever."

"No, I mean, before you knew there were time travelers." I ask.

"Oh, ok. Yeah, all the time. I think we all do. It's just built into us, see? Being in your twenties is new to you when you're a teenager and being in your thirties is new to you when you are in your twenties, etcetera, etcetera. Understand?"

"Yeah. It's just hard, ya know. I mean, it's hard enough being a teenager and like, all the drama we go through. We put ourselves through it. But what we think is so important won't even matter one iota a week from now. And look at this. We are standing on the threshold of inhalation. Now this, this my friend, is true drama."

"Ha ha, yeah, Jon. So, you don't have to give me specifics of times and names but, can you tell me what the future will be like?"

We continue to drive through the night. I look at the back bench seat and see that Abby and

Pete have both fallen asleep. They are propped up on each other like a deck of cards, each one holding the other one up. I really think they'll end up going out together one day. Not anytime soon, but in the near future. If we make it, that is.

I decide it's ok to tell Chuck about some events. I mean, it's just like a preview right? It won't hurt to just, let him in on a couple of things. Will it?

"Ok, I can tell you a few things. Or, is there some specific topic you wanted to know about?"

"No, just anything, pal, anything at all."

Where to start? I mean, Wow! The world has seen so much happen since the forties. So many positives and, of course, negatives.

I tell him about the Cold War, the Space Race and ultimate landing on the moon. I tell him about the popularity of color TVs in our homes, how records are replaced by eight tracks, by tapes, by cds and now by directly downloading digital files. Downloading digital files opens up a different can of worms which leads me to the internet and how all of our personal data is stored electronically. I tell him to buy a copy of George Orwell's classic, *1984*, and that our life is eerily similar to that. But then realize the book won't be out 'till the end of this decade. 1949, I believe?

I describe other wars, dictators and the rise of terrorism. About how it's not safe to be certain places at certain times of the night which he says is already true in his present time. I add that you can't leave your house or your car unlocked. I tell him about the rise of alcohol and recreational drug use. I tell him about the genocides, the atomic age, the fear, the disease, the starvation.

Wow, this is depressing me. Why am I even so anxious to get back to my day and age?

"Is there anything good about the future?" he asks. I ask myself that same question. Then, I realize there is.

I apologize to Chuck for all the gloom and doom and switch to happier thoughts. I respond to his question with one word: family. Family is always there and never changes and is always safe. My faith and God are always there too. So, yes, some things do stay the same and are not tarnished at all.

"Don't get me wrong," I say. "There are many other great things, too. Cures for diseases, faster, safer, easier and more efficient ways of doing things. Like, in my normal life in my time, it would be considered regular, but to you guys it would probably be really luxurious. Everything is automatic but it's also disposable which means that things are not the best quality as they used to be. Take this car for instance. This thing, if taken care of, will last forever, not to mention the body style. Most cars in my time are just, I dunno, pretty plain. There are some cool ones but you will never see a station wagon from my day end up at a car show, ya know what I mean?

"Not really." Chuck seems like he enjoys the

concept. He pushes hard on the pedal and shifts again as we rumble down the barren tropical highway.

As we pass wide open spaces speckled with palm trees and little shanties, I continue telling Chuck about video games and microwave ovens. I take a closer look at the little huts as they fly by the window. They obviously belong to the native islanders and have been here well before the Americans arrived. Honestly, this area is kind of familiar. I think it's where Pete and I first arrived.

"What's that up ahead?" I ask.

There are some lights down the road in the distance. As we get closer I can see that the lights are actually from police cars, brightening up the area with their huge roof mounted red lights. Chuck slows down as we approach.

We get closer and see the two police cars parked along the shoulder. Off to the side of the road is a very familiar looking black sedan. It rests, grill first, in a ditch. Three officers shine flashlights into it while another one stands outside of his car, on the police radio. They hardly notice us at all.

Chuck drives past the action and slows down a bit to get a better look.

"That's their car alright. I remember that dent on the rear fender. Although there are a lot more dents on it now," says Chuck. Pete and Abby are still asleep in the back. They are knocked out.

CHAPTER FOURTEEN

We continue our journey to the North Shore. Chuck gradually accelerates and drives us away from the scene. But before we get going, the barrel of a gun is shoved through the window and is now pointed right at me. All I see is the gun and an outstretched arm. I look out the window to find Jackson's cruel sneer being lowered into sight as he peeks into the Woody. He reaches in with his other hand in an effort to unlock the door. All the while he is still holding the gun on me, brushing the cold steel against my nose.

"Hold on, Jon!" Chuck demands.

"No, Chuck! Don't drive! Don't drive! Please!" Trying to drive off with a gun aimed at me is not the best move right now.

"Yeah, kid. Don't even try it." That's probably the only thing on which Jackson and I will ever agree.

He opens the door from the inside and enters, squeezing his way in along the front bench seat and plopping down right next to me. He is injured from

135

the police shootout and, besides blood, he is now covered with dirt and debris. He grabs the door and quietly pulls it shut in order to avoid making any sound.

I glance back at the police to find them down in the ditch, still looking around the black sedan. I can't believe we are this close to the cops and are being jacked.

"Drive!" commands Jackson. But we just sit there. Chuck is still staring at the gun aimed directly at me.

"Drive! Now!" Jackson commands again. Chuck presses on the gas and slowly gets going. He should actually burn rubber to draw some attention from the cops, but in all honestly, I am glad that he doesn't. My expression thanks him.

We drive up and over a hill when Jackson tells us to pull over. I am surprised that he doesn't order us out, shoot us and steal the car. Instead, he waves his hand towards the side of a small temple. Right before the temple is a tall gate. I have seen one before, kind of traditional, Asian-like architecture. I can't remember if it's Buddhist or Shinto or what.

Klara steps out from the gate's right pillar. She is holding a very large black bag. Jackson continues to wave her on as she slowly creeps over. She hunches to keep her cover as best as she is able.

"Come on, Come on!" Jackson yells.

Pete and Abby, are awaken by this new commotion. Klara opens the door and gets in the car.

Pete puts himself between Abby and Klara as she gets into the back seat.

"Well, well, we meet again little children." Klara takes a long glance at Chuck and says, "And you, the driver, you are not so little are you? You are a big boy." She smiles a sexy smile at Chuck.

Jackson motions to the windshield with his gun and directs us to get going. We start back up, all six of us. It wouldn't be that bad. I mean this wagon is huge, but we don't want to be any closer than we have to be to these characters. Right now defines the phrase, 'too close for comfort.'

"Where are we going exactly?" Chuck asks as he continues to drive ahead, without taking his eyes off of the road.

"Don't play stupid, island boy. You know exactly where we are headed," Klara says as she glances over towards Abby, an obvious sign that she knows Abby had ample time to observe and memorize the many maps at their hideout.

"North Shore it is then." says Chuck.

"Yeah, but can we finally know why? Just what is so important?" I ask.

Klara looks at me and squints. She follows it up with a smile, not as ominous a smile as Jackson, but an evil smile nonetheless.

"That is for me to know and you to find out. And, you will find out soon enough my little friend," she says, in her thick German accent, "You will find out soon enough."

137

"Gee, thanks, 'cuz that's not an extremely creepy thing to say. Are you at least from our time, like the twenty-first century?"

"Yes, that much I will tell you. I am from your time, the time that is familiar to you. Jackson on the other hand is a totally different story."

I kind of figured as much. That guy was loopy. I don't just mean that in the, "he is a psychopath, crazed, lunatic" type of way. I mean he is just . . . off. You can tell he isn't exactly from our era, even though he is American. Or, at least I think he is. Who knows with these two?

"Just relax, children. It will all be over shortly. Keep driving to your favorite surfing area, island boy."

"Yes, ma'am," Chuck replies sarcastically. He is greeted with Jackson's gun barrel aiming square at him. Chuck smiles.

The car is once again dead silent. Everyone is wide awake, but something about two strangers in your car, barking out orders and one holding a weapon, does something to the desire to talk. Besides, Klara already said we will find out "soon enough." I am not sure what that means but I am sure it will be answered when we reach the North Shore. I think she watched too many movies growing up. She might as well have said her favorite line again, "That is for me to know and you to find out."

We drive for another fifteen minutes until Chuck says, "Ok, here we are. What's next,

Gertrude?" Chuck is pushing it. But I love every minute of it.

"I told you! My name is Klara, Klara Beich! And don't you forget it, young man. My name may not be in the history books for this, but it will be there nonetheless, that is for sure. Mark my words. Now, turn up ahead at that plantation shack."

For the first time, Klara actually looks flustered, like she has been put in her place. Nice job, Chuck.

Chuck drives us ahead as instructed. Pete and Abby are in the back, both staring at Klara, studying and watching her every move and expression as she speaks. I, on the other hand, have to fight for space crammed in-between Chuck, the hero and Jackson, the villain, on the long, old bench seat of the Woody.

Chuck makes a left onto a very bumpy dirt road that leads to the shore. He hits a huge dip and then another.

"Dude, please!" I stress.

"Sorry, buddy." says Chuck.

"Well, you are gonna be more sorry if one of those bumps makes his gun go off at my head!" Chuck raises his eyebrows in an acceptance of guilt and apology. He regains his calm posture as another sense of the reality of the situation washes over him.

"There! Over there by the shanties." Klara points over at what seems to be an abandoned village full of little shacks and huts, reminiscent of a Hooverville poster my teacher had in his classroom a few years back.

She gives further instructions to drive to the shack nearest the dirt road. Even though I figured it out already, Chuck whispers that this is not his usual North Shore surfing destination. The wooden buildings are deeply enveloped in and around palm trees and other indigenous flora. No electrical lights can be seen at all. Either this place is totally abandoned or the inhabitants still use candles, oil or simple torch lights, none of which can be seen right now.

Chuck applies the brakes and puts the car in park. We sit, idling while awaiting further instructions. The gun is still pressed against my right temple.

"Why haven't you killed us already?" asks Pete brazenly.

"Pete!" I cry, "What the hell, man?"

"Well, we are all thinking it," Chuck honestly admits.

Klara opens the door, steps out of the car and turns back towards Pete.

"All in good time, Pete, all in good time. I still want you, all of you, to know what's happening. Plus, a little insurance never hurt."

'All in good time?' How many idioms does this chick have?

Jackson also exits the car, carefully. He keeps his gun aimed at me, while backing up and watching his feet on the choppy dirt path. He directs

140

us to get out of the car.

Chuck exits first, via his driver's side door. I slide over towards Chuck's door to exit but then notice something on the floor where Jackson was sitting. I change the direction of my exit and instead go towards Jackson.

I scoot over the long bench seat, as if reaching for the collection basket at church. I spot the item. It's stuck under the floor panel and is hidden by Jackson's moon-cast shadow. It's his cigarette box, the one that shot the orange acid at the cop at Diamond Head.

I keep sliding out of the car and before I exit, I back heel the box towards Chuck on the other side of the car. At least I learned one soccer move from Abby! Chuck sees it but cautiously waits for the right moment to pick it up.

"Out! Now! We don't have all night, kiddies," says Klara. Pete and Abby slowly get out on the same side as I. I look over towards them, nod my head and mouth the words, "It's ok." They wouldn't be foolish enough to run now anyways, not with Jackson still clutching his piece.

Chuck sees Pete and Abby's exit as his opportunity. He bends over and picks up the cigarette box.

"Watch it, kid!" shouts Jackson as he repositions his weapon on Chuck.

"Whoa now, John Wayne, just lacing up my shoe!"

141

Chuck picks up the cigarette box and sticks it under his sock band while pretending to tie his shoe. Jackson's view is obstructed by the body of the Woody. Chuck walks over to our side of the car and joins the rest of us.

Jackson motions for us to step away from the car. Klara is now preoccupied, starring down the road we just turned off of. She leans over to Jackson, without looking at him and says, "They should be here shortly." She turns around and walks back towards us.

"Everyone have a seat," she says as she walks past us, towards a wooden picnic table. She pauses, takes another look down the road, then sits at the table.

"Come on kids," directs Jackson. We reluctantly follow. We could easily escape, one at a time, but not all at once. We are not gagged or tied up or anything. I guess their time table does not allow for it. Jackson does have that gun, after all. One or more of us would definitely not make it.

"So now what?" asks Pete.

"Now we wait for the help to arrive." answers Jackson, in his usual gruff voice.

"The help?" asks Abby.

Klara gets up from the picnic table bench, and instead, sits on the table itself. She leans back, her arms supporting her, and stares at the night sky.

"Alright, children, I suppose while we are waiting for reinforcements, I might as well explain

142

everything," she says as she pushes herself out of her reclined position. "Sounds good? Ok, good."

"Yes, please tell us what all this is about! Why here? Why now?" I demand as we sit down at the table.

CHAPTER FIFTEEN

"I was about to tell you when we were so rudely interrupted by that police officer. Anyhow, we are going to do our best to prevent the attack from happening in the morning."

"What? How do you think you can do that?" Pete asks.

"How? Who cares?" Chuck asks, "Maybe these guys aren't as bad as we thought? They want to prevent the attack, didn't you hear her?"

"NO!" Abby breaks her silence. "That can't be done. Pearl Harbor *has* to be attacked." I feel like Abby is the only one who understands how dire the situation really is.

"She's right! The surprise attack on Pearl Harbor is one of the most important events in American, no, no, in World History! It must happen! The changes it would create would be devastating. Who knows what the world would be like in our time if Pearl was never attacked. I know it sounds crazy, but it's true!"

"That is exactly why we are going to do it!" Klara pounds her fist on the table.

"Oh. For a minute there I thought you cared about saving America." Chuck says with a frown on his face.

"Never! I hate America! Hate it!" She pounds the table again, harder than before.

Abby and Pete back away from Klara as much as they can without getting up from the table.

"Sorry, kids." Jackson says, "She gets a little impassioned and emotional about this whole thing. Ya see, it all started when . . ."

"No!" Klara interrupts Jackson. "I will tell them the story." Klara glances over at the road. Still nothing.

"It starts with my grandfather, Dietrich von Wexler. He was one of Germany's most brilliant and talented scientists, top of his class and the Fuehrer's favorite! He was going to help Germany win the war. He would have done it, too, but Hitler was so entranced, so mesmerized with far off, wild theories on the fringe of science, that he had ordered my grandfather, the best scientist there, to move in another direction."

I don't know the full story yet, but right now, she is demonstrating the most human characteristics she has ever shown. She is not teary eyed, nor is she sniffling. I am guessing she has already gone through this story many times in the past.

"And what direction was that?" Abby asks.

Pete leans to Abby and under his breath says, "Losing the war, no doubt, ha ha."

145

"Actually, you are right." Klara says, matter of factly.

Pete faces me and nods. Lucky guess of course. But how was he right?

"Because Grandpa Dietrich wanted to stick with it, to continue his nuclear program. He was so close, so close to harnessing the power of the atom."

"Not close enough, 'cuz we beat the Nazis without even having to use the bomb!"

"Pete! That's enough," I chastise.

"Yes, once again you impetuous little boy, you are correct. He was close, that is, until Hitler wanted him to start working on other things."

"Like what?"

"Like a cloaking device, matter transporter, alchemy, a sound canon, a bomber in space, anything and everything out of the ordinary. Grandpa knew these were definitely interesting fields of study, but he also knew that there was no time for it. The Germans were in a two front war and Hitler had him working on fantasy instead of his main focus which was the nuclear program. And yes, we would have had the bomb way ahead of the Americans if it wasn't for Hitler's wild dreams."

"So wait a minute," says Abby, "that's all sad and everything, but just where does America fit into all of this? Why blame it on the U.S. when you seem to realize it was the Germans' fault that sealed your grandfather's fate. If Hitler would have let your grandfather continue his program, Germany would have had the nuke way before anyone else and could have, well, ruled the world."

"It is America's fault because it was America who tried Grandpa at the Nuremburg trials! He begged and pleaded and attempted to make a deal with them. He even offered the United States his greatest inventions in return for his freedom. But they refused! It was America who denied my grandpa to be free. And in doing so they could have had all the power in the world!" Klara begins to tear up but quickly wipes them away.

"Yeah, but were any of the inventions ever realized? I mean, were any of them any good?" Pete asks.

"Are you stupid? Klara questions. "You live in the twenty-first century and right now you're in 1941. These things mean anything to you?" she says as she removes the temporal devices from her bag and presents them.

"The United States claimed neutrality once again. They didn't want to enter the war. Well, this time I will make sure that comes true!"

"Settle down, Klara, come on now. Don't lose your cool," Jackson, the workhorse, says in the most soothing manner we've seen yet. He walks up to Klara and places his right hand on the collar of her jacket.

She places her worn out hands on her face and begins to sob. She pulls away from Jackson, gets off of the table and walks towards the closest shanty.

147

Jackson stays with us, his gun a little less aimed and positioned but still at the ready if need be. He leans over, one foot upon the bench and hands on his upright knee, and says. "Well, I guess this is where I finish the story."

"You know the rest?" Chuck asks.

"I should," Jackson retorts, "I have heard it about a billion times. Jackson pauses and stares directly into our eyes before continuing the story.

"So, her grandfather offered everything to the U.S. Even Einstein had wanted to work with von Wexler. His theories and ideas were off the charts, kid. And like she said, we are living proof of it."

"So, forgive me, but I am new to all of this since I am actually from the present and not the past or the future," Chuck says. "But why are you trying to help America out?"

"That's easy, see kid. If America doesn't enter the war, Germany will win and take over Europe. That means America won't have the Nuremburg trials, and Klara's gramps won't hafta die, see?

"And, he will also have time to continue his atomic program." Abby chimes in.

"But why this? I mean . . . why not just save her grandfather another way? Why not go back in time and free him from prison, or convince Hitler to let him spend more time on the nuclear program or, I mean, there are countless other ways." insists Abby.

"Why not, kid? Why not? That's the plan.

148

Germany is where it's at. With the U.S. out of the picture, Klara's home country wins the game, grandpa lives, and it ensures the safety of Germany without having to go nuclear. Plus the time devices can be improved. They have a lot of bugs to be worked out." Jackson glances back at Klara.

"We *did* actually try other things. Easier scenarios, like you said. They wouldn't have changed much in the overall scheme of things, really. But none of them worked." Jackson confesses.

"Like what," asks Pete leaning in closer.

"Something always went wrong and we had to go back again and again and keep correcting it. We went back the night before the trial to try to bust him out, but one of his own cellmates squealed on him. We went back to when he was captured and one of our own men got captured instead and threw off the whole plan. Another time, we entered the wrong coordinates and landed in Normandy on D-Day! Stupid Leo!"

"What's Normandy? What's D-day? What's that?" questions Chuck.

Jackson continues without answering Chuck, "One thing changed, then another and another and another. Only it wasn't the thing Klara wanted changed. She lost old gramps every single time. She figures now if we do something much earlier and even prevent the U.S. from joining the war, her grandfather will have the best chance to survive. You have to admit it, kids, she loves her family."

149

"True, but that doesn't make her any less crazy. She's out there! Sorry you are with her. Are you two married or what? I mean . . . why are you helping her do all this?" I ask.

"Naw, naw, we're not together. Yeah, she is a crazy thing but, hey, she pays good and I'm guaranteed safety no matter what happens. I owe her. She sprung me from a federal pen back in the thirties. I was public enemy number one, after Dillinger, that is."

So that's how Jackson fits in. He is just a hired thug after all, only from a different time.

Jackson looks up as we all hear cars traveling down the road.

"Story time is over, kids. And, oh, she is only keepin' you all alive to watch the show." Jackson stands up, climbs onto the top of the wagon and raises his hands to his mouth like an announcer. "To see tonight's main event: The reverse Pearl Harbor invasion. Just call it, 'Klara's revenge on America by way of the Japanese.' Ahahahaha!"

I don't know which one of these characters is more eccentric, Klara, the crazed Nazi sympathizer or Jackson, the screamo-sounding henchmen.

"They are here!" Klara shouts at the sight of four rumbling pickup trucks loaded with men. These are undoubtedly the reinforcements we were waiting for.

The trucks pull up alongside the Woody. They each have around ten guys piled into the back. I wonder if they were all former prisoners as well. Did Klara go around to the past decades and handpick her criminal team?

Probably not. Upon further inspection, they look nothing like the highly tailored Jackson. If this was a handpicked crew, she must have gotten a bargain because this group is more rag-tag then the two of them. Most of them are in simple t-shirts and dungarees.

"Ok, children, back into the car. We must get closer to the shore," says Klara while waving the trucks past us and towards and old pier about three hundred yards away.

Jackson goes back to his usual fashion of sticking his gun into our backs and directing us into the car. We pile in like cows being led to slaughter. This time, however, Klara decides to take the wheel.

She sits in the driver's position and starts the engine. Chuck had left the keys in the ignition. I guess he was hoping for a chance to make a break for it. We head over toward the pier. No doubt all of us are wondering just how Klara thinks she will stop the massive Japanese fleet of six aircraft carriers and all of their planes.

We get to the pier just as the final truck arrives and pulls in behind us. All the men jump out of the trucks and start to look around as if they are new to this. One at a time, we step out of the Woody. Chuck lifts up his shirttail and shows me that he still has the cigarette box contraption of Jackson's. It is tucked safely under his belt.

"Ok, everyone, once the job is over you will get your fair share of pay that you were promised. There will be about three to five people on every vessel. We have no time to spare! You were all given your orders earlier. Please do not try to deviate from them."

"What does she mean, Jon?" Pete whispers to me and the others. "There are no vessels here. No ships, no boats, no raft, not even a simple dinghy."

The men seem as confused as we are. They are looking towards the water, the pier and some are even looking back towards the old shacks. There is nothing here at all. I knew Klara was crazy, but this is ridiculous.

"Ahem!" mutters Jackson as he points out at the emptiness of the water. Klara glances over and says, "Oh, where is my bag? How foolish of me!"

Jackson reaches into the driver seat and pulls out the German's big bag.

"Ok . . . here, here we are," she says as she rummages through the bag. "No, no, that's not it." She empties the contents of the bag on the Woody's massive hood. About fifteen to twenty little trinkets and gadgets appear, including the two time devices. We have got to get them back. But it would be harder now than ever with so many people on their payroll.

"Here we are," she says as she picks up one of the items, a silver cylinder filled with a green fluid.

152

She walks over towards the ocean and holds the cylinder in air. She looks over at me and says, "This is another one of Grandpa's inventions. Like the temporal device, he never got to see it realized. But with his blue print masterpiece and schematics, we have realized his vision for him!"

The top of the stick opens up like an old-fashioned, rabbit-eared, TV antenna and starts spinning around. She pushes the only button on the item and a giant, green umbrella of light showers across the night sky. It looks like a million lightning bugs were just released, simultaneously illuminating the entire area.

As the green haze falls to the ground, it reveals a harbor full of boats. There are about fifteen of them, each around forty feet in length. They honestly remind me of the PT-109, the Patrol Torpedo boat that Kennedy was aboard during the war. The only difference was, these did not have any military insignia on them, whatsoever. They were painted jet black, no doubt to camouflage them in the dark of the ocean.

In the back of each boat are three huge wooden crates, simply labeled: *Live Explosives*. Each boat also has a forward and rear mounted gun. I am not sure of the caliber, but believe me, they are massive. They could definitely create some damage in the hull of a Japanese carrier, if that's what she was really planning. But was it enough to bring down the entire fleet?

Abby, Chuck, Pete and I stand in awe. Of course traveling in time was a major feat in itself, but this, this is just incredible!

"Did you just create those ships with that magic wand thing," asks Chuck.

"Ha ha ha," Klara laughs. "No, silly islander, they were there all the time. The magic wand, as you call it, simply lifted the protective shield. You see, it prevents anyone from seeing them and also prevents any damage. That is how we will defeat the Japanese and prevent the attack on Pearl Harbor. We will simply pop up and destroy the Japanese!"

The men start to board the ships. They also bring along some other crates from the trucks. I assume it is more ammo.

"What do you mean, 'pop up'?" asks Chuck.

"Well, we will use a temporal device to bend space and time just a little bit. Since we are at the right time, and not so many nautical miles away, it will be a piece of cake.

"So you use the same time travel device?

"No, it is a different type, more like a matter transporter. Not as powerful as the other devices but quite impressive nonetheless. We'll surround the Japanese and open fire. And if they break through our line, we have an ocean full of mines. They will not know what hit them!"

"Well, well, good job. But you forgot one thing," says Pete with an air of an unjustified upper hand. "What about the mini subs! Some of those were the first ones to attack. They have to be on their way already!" Pete looks over at me with an anxious expression and says, "Back me up on this, Jon!"

"Don't worry, they are being taken care of," Klara says. She points over towards the last truck where six of the men are putting on modern-looking wet suits. At the back of the truck is a trailer that carries, what appears to be their own, two man, minisub. But this sub looks very modern. It reminds me of a submarine that was given away on a game show not too long ago, very sleek and seemingly very fast. There are also two torpedo tubes along the sides - formidable opponents to the Japanese mini subs of the early forties.

They really seem to have everything planned out this time. I don't know if it will work or not, but I don't see any reason as to why it wouldn't. They have the manpower, the firepower and they definitely have the technological advantage. I wonder what other kind of crazy mad scientist inventions Grandpa Dietrich had come up with. Maybe that Dr. Jekyll and Mr. Hyde movie wasn't too far off.

"Everyone! Get on your boat, right now!" yells Klara."Blue team is going to the right and Red team is to the left. We will sail for 300 yards and then I will reactivate the shield and launch us to the Japanese coordinates. Remember, as soon as we get there, open fire. Your eyes will be a little blurry due to the transport, but once things clear up, open fire. Unload everything we have on them." She takes a breath, cracks a smile and continues.

"Thanks to some early prep work from our wetsuit crew," she says while gesturing towards the men, "one plane on each of the six carriers is already loaded with explosives. I will detonate them during the attack. Your job is to prevent any other aircraft from leaving. Is that totally clear?"

The crowd of, shall I say, "volunteers," responds with a collective grunt and finish getting on their assigned boats. Everyone is at their post and ready to go. That is to say, everyone but us.

Jackson herds us closer together and motions for us to sit in the back of the nearest boat. We shuffle onboard as the boat shifts back and forth in the water. Jackson and Klara join us.

This boat is different than the others. It's still jet black with no writing on it, but it's much smaller than the other boats and surprisingly enough, doesn't have any weapons. It doesn't even have life vests or anything. All it has is Klara's big bag and a detonator. It must be rigged to some of the planes on the carriers like she had mentioned.

Jackson heads to the rear of the boat, leans over and starts the two outboard motors. He comes up with motor oil and grime covering his hands. He reaches over towards Chuck, grabs him by his shirt and begins using Chuck's shirt as a mechanic's rag.

Chuck gets to his feet and pushes Jackson causing him to lose his balance. He falls backward toward the edge of the boat but catches himself quickly. Klara shakes her head back and forth in apparent disgust of Jackson. He steps forward, draws his gun and aims it right at Chuck.

"Let me off this one right now, Klara! Come on!" Jackson says with an ever-widening grin.

"No. Just sit down, shut up and control them. They need to see this. They need to see history being rewritten! All of them!"

Jackson regains his composure and sits down. Klara stands on her tippy toes, gives everyone the "let's go" signal of both arms waving in the air, and the boats begin to move forward.

"Jon, we gotta do something," Abby whispers. "We can't let the attack on Pearl Harbor *not* happen."

"I don't know what we can do, Abby. I just don't know."

Is there honestly anything we *can* do? It's such an odd predicament to be in. We know the surprise attack of Pearl Harbor has to happen. We *have* to be bombed or the outcome of the war, well, it might just go the way she wants it to, with Germany dominating the Eastern Hemisphere. But at the same time, I have a flashback of the little boy with his mother at the toy store window. Their lives, their hopes, their families, all of that will be turned upside down.

But I guess . . . I guess what has happened is what *must* happen. No matter how sad it may be. It doesn't matter. The ball is in their court. The fate of the world is in Klara's hands now. I am out of ideas.

The boats launch from the pier, one by one, taking up a triangular shape, reminiscent of geese flying south for the winter. I wonder about the men on the other boats.

"So, who are all of these guys anyways?" I ask Klara.

"Nobody special, really. None of them are soldiers of course; they are either too old, too young, too unfit, etcetera, etcetera. They only know the basics. I simply told them that the Japanese are too close to American soil and we must attack them before they attack us. I told them the U.S. military was too incompetent to attack preemptively so instead, I formed my own private militia. I will kill two birds with one stone as they say: they get money for working for me and also feel like they are helping defend America. The majority, however are sympathetic to the German cause."

"You mean the Nazi cause"

"Yes, yes. One in the same."

"I didn't know there was such a large German population in Hawaii." comments Abby.

"No, there isn't. I have recruited them from the east coast, mainly in the New England area. You know the type. They come to America looking for opportunity and the American dream, but end up living in the slums of the cities. And because of the depression, oh, please, it was too easy to find these men. They were hit hard and never recovered. It did

158

not take much. We just had to feed them and their families."

"So they think they are out saving the day for Hitler, huh . . . to give him a better chance?"

"As I said, some of them. But yes, they *are* out saving the day! They will be heroes! Hitler himself should thank them, should thank all of us. But of course, not even Hitler will know what we have done for the glory of Germany."

"You do realize that, just because you prevent this attack from happening, doesn't mean that America will never join the war? You are just postponing it at best. The Japanese will try to attack again, or somewhere else, and even if they don't, the U.S. is already assisting the British with so many different programs like Lend Lease." I insist.

"Postpone is the key word my friend. Even if it only postpones the U.S. entry into the war, for say, a few months, that will be three months Germany didn't have before. The Nazis will defeat the Soviets now, full force. They will not have to split their forces on two fronts. There will be no "defeat Hitler first" strategy. No, this time we will do it. This will be it. I will finally get to know my grandfather and with his inventions and ideas, the Third Reich will reign for a thousand years!"

I lean back, along the side of the boat. Abby rests her head on my shoulder. If this were any other time, I would have shooed her off immediately. But for some reason, now, I don't even care that she ever had a crush on me. For all I know, these are likely our last moments together. Our lasts moments . . . period!

CHAPTER SIXTEEN

"Hey," Klara says, "My turn to question you. How long did it take you to find the device after you made it here? You know, it always gets thrown from my hand during travel. It emits such power and energy we totally lose control of it. The thermal switch is the culprit, I believe."

"Yeah, you think your grandfather would have done a better job on that one." Pete admonishes.

"You listen to me you little twerp. Did you grandfather come up with time travel? Hmmm. Well? Did he? I didn't think so."

Klara has a very complaisant smile. She is right, after all. To achieve time travel with such a minor flaw is a great accomplishment.

"Yes, I know, we need to fix it. But once again, this was his last project. He never really perfected it. Had Hitler let him work on the atomic program the American pigs would not have won the war and would not have executed him. They could have made a deal. Just think of the possibilities."

161

She is so stupid. Her grandfather, of course, was her blood, her family, her heritage, but he was still one other thing: he was a Nazi. And even if it meant death, he could have refused to work for them. *That* at least would be a more noble and honorable way to die. God only knows what kind of experiments he performed on people. But I am not gonna play that card again. Klara will just lose control. I better answer her question.

"Yeah, well, it was easy to find. At least, easier than it was for you guys, losing it in our neighborhood and such. I mean, we had a wide open area to search through. You had private property in our neighborhood with meddling kids, like us." I laugh.

"Yes, with meddling kids," she says. "It would have been much easier if Jackson's hired helpers weren't so incompetent. Little stubby man is no good. Useless I tell you. Why would they ever choose such a highly occupied place to transmit from?" she says while directing her words towards Jackson. Jackson just sits there wiping off some dirt from his top dollar shoes.

"Well, ours wasn't half as hard as it was to find yours. It was only a few yards away near some palm trees." I explain.

"That is because there were only two of you. We took all of us. The more people you take, the more energy it needs and the further it goes from its hosts. Yes, there are some bugs to diffuse but we will make modifications when we have time. Now if you do not mind, I must focus and get back to work. Sit back and enjoy the show."

We continue to sail away from the harbor, approaching our 300 yard destination. Klara halts our vessel and with her hands, makes a slowing down signal to the other ships. One by one, they near our lead boat. The engines quiet down to a whispering idle.

Jackson grabs Klara's bag, walks aft and hands it to her. She rummages through it. I am surprised that anything works at all. It's like packing your Christmas ornaments in a box without any bubble wrap or Styrofoam peanuts and then kicking it as hard as you can. She has these one of a kind inventions and simply stores them in an oversized bag. Typical dumb criminal I suppose: ingenious plans laid with the foundation of basic stupidity.

She empties the contents on the floor of the boat, obviously in an ill-tempered, chaotic state of mind. She finally finds the one she is looking for. She takes the metal item and connects it to, the cloaking one, the one that revealed all of the ships at the pier.

"Everyone ready?" Klara shouts while holding the two items, still connected, but one in each hand. She flips the switch on the cloaking device and the three little antennas once again spring up and start to spiral around each other. The green haze begins to reappear above us. The light of the green haze illuminates our ship as well as those surrounding us,

163

bathing us in its eeriness.

"It is time! Gather together!" They are almost fully powered now! Yes! Yes!" she cries with madness. "We are just about there. Get ready! Man your weapons!"

I am not sure what is about to happen but it can't be good. "You guys hold on and take cover!" I tell Pete and Abby as I grab hold to the side railing of the boat. I have no reason as to why, but Chuck is looking behind the action, behind us, off to the West.

"Chuck! Hold on, man! Take cover! We don't know what she's up to! Get down!" He is still starring behind us, squeezing his eyes tightly as the veil of green continues to encompass us.

"What is it? What is it?" I ask.

"Look, Jon!"

I examine the direction of Chuck's focus and sure enough a small light appears, then another and another. They are really hard to see through the green light that completely surrounds us. I can faintly hear the sound of more boat engines in the distance. Klara and Jackson are so focused on their process that they do not see or hear what we do. Some of the hired help, however, start to take notice of the sounds of engines rumbling in the not so distant westward horizon of the night sky. Abby and Pete start to take notice as well.

"Get ready! 25% more power and then we activate!" Klara still doesn't see or hear whatever or whoever is approaching us. Or maybe they are a part of her plan? Will they reach us when her devices are at full capacity? Maybe she was waiting for them the whole time?

The lights become clearer and the engines roar. They are coming at full speed now. I still can't make out who or what it is. Are the lights from Japanese scouts sent ahead to make sure everything is prepped for the attack? Maybe I misunderstood Klara and we are already approaching the carriers?

But no. The lights, the engines and the vessels to which they belong come closer into view. It is not the Japanese, nor is it local fishermen. It's nothing less than the Coast Guard! The ships, four of them, fly up behind our wake and with their massive spot lights, signal us to stop. A voice comes across a loud horn saying, "Cut the engines and put your hands up! This is the United States Coast Guard!"

Klara and Jackson are no longer preoccupied with the shielding device. Most of our ships reduce speed and come to a slow pace but continue to maintain their current heading.

Once again the voice comes across the speaker: "Unauthorized vessels, cease and desist. Put your hands on your heads!"

Following the announced commands, the rest of the gunships cut their engines. Several more Coast Guard ships come from the right and cut directly in our path.

Jackson averts disaster by sharply turning the boat starboard. Klara is thrown to the grown and the device falls from her hand and lands in the choppy waters beneath us. The green lighted haze gradually dissipates, like a lighting strike in slow motion, backing off from its strike zone.

Jackson is also thrown to the ground. He is able to maintain one of his hands on the wheel and pulls himself back up, but he is missing something: his gun. He frantically searches the floor of the ship, as do we. First one to the gun is the winner. It is, after all, foolishly, the only practical weapon onboard.

And there, in the gleam of the ocean, the silver barrel glimmers in the night. It's directly under Chuck's seat. Risking Klara and Jackson hearing me, I scream, "CHUCK!" as I point to the gun. Klara is once again, preoccupied. This time she is leaning over the edge of the boat with a net, trying to fish for her protective shield device. The Coast Guard cutters seem to be enjoying the show as they highlight every movement with their massive spotlights.

Chuck sees the gun and reaches over to snatch it up, but Jackson is too quick. With both hands, he grabs hold of Chuck's head and slams him to the ground. Jackson pushes off of the boat wheel and crawls over Chuck, shoving him to the side.

The ship sways the other way and the gun slides down the floor to Abby's feet. Jackson gets up and heads towards it. The Coast Guard spotlights are shining everywhere back and forth, all over the place as another announcement is made commanding all of us to stop our movements.

"Get it, Abb! Get it!" cries Pete.

Abby reaches down to retrieve the gun and succeeds in doing so. Jackson lunges towards her, grabs her and begins to pry her fingers off of the gun. She tries to fight for it. They sway to the left and right, both holding the gun in the air. Abby just can't hold on. Jackson finally wins and gets the gun. Then out of nowhere Jackson screams, "Ahhhhhhhh!" He drops the gun and reaches for his eyes. Abby quickly recovers the revolver and steadily holds it on him.

Chuck stands across from Jackson. He had sprayed Jackson with the fake cigarette box that we retrieved earlier! The orange acid oozes over Jackson's head as he thrusts his body to the edge of the boat and begins to splash water on his face in hope of some relief. "Who is the tough guy now, buddy?" Abby says as she aims the pistol at Jackson, in an empowering moment of revenge.

"Here, Abby, I better take that," says Chuck, slowly reaching over and retrieving the gun from Abby while still keeping it aimed on Jackson.

Klara, still hunched over the side with her fishing net in a last ditch attempt to scoop up her two, combined devices, turns back and is greeted by a Coast Guard officer who has just boarded our ship. He reaches behind his belt, takes out his cuffs and begins to cuff her. She looks back at Jackson and says, "Nice move, Jackson! I told you I did not like that blasted acid box! Nothing but trouble!" Jackson, now wiping off the orange residue from his face with his high quality button up shirt, shrugs and admits defeat.

"An invention of your grandfather's that you don't like huh, Klara?" asks Abby.

"That stupid thing? Oh, please child. You are comparing that with the greatness of my opa? He did not make that! That is one of Jackson's very own."

"Jackson made it?"

"Yeah, don't look so surprised, kid," Jackson says as another officer pushes him to the ground and frisks him. "Sure it's nothing like hers, but hey, it broke me outta prison three times! Just a little squirt on the cell lock and presto!"

"Nice," says Abby, "Now it has broken your face out!"

Jackson growls at Abby. "If my face is messed up I promise you, you little . . ."

"That's enough out of you, buddy," says the officer, cutting Jackson off, mid-threat.

The rest of the boats are boarded without struggle. All of Klara's hired help heed the instructions, interlock their hands and place them on their heads. One by one they are frisked, handcuffed and transported to the larger white, bright, shiny Coast Guard cutters. The defeated men cross from one boat to the next via a simple plank of wood.

"I say we should just let them walk the plank and swim with the fishes," says Pete in a New York accent.

Klara is last to be taken across. The captain

himself brings her to her feet, holding her by her handcuffed hands.

"You must stop them! They are going to attack you! They are coming soon! They are coming!!"

"No, lady," the captain says, "They are not coming. We just stopped them, all of them, see?" He points over to Klara's former crew, now handcuffed on the Coast Guard ships.

"No, not them . . . not . . . not us, the Japanese! The Japanese are going to bomb Pearl Harbor! They are going to launch a surprise attack at daybreak!"

"Oh, the Japanese, huh?" questions the captain.

"I suppose they were out to stop them huh, Cap'n?" says a bright eyed seaman.

"I suppose so Seaman Richards, I suppose so." They both chuckle.

"No, we *were* going to stop them! They must be stopped! They must be stopped at all costs!"

"Sure, lady. You were gonna stop the Japanese navy with a couple little boats and guns huh? The Japanese aren't even at war with us, you loopy broad. They've got diplomats in Washington right now working things out. I even got news a little while ago that Roosevelt himself sent that Emperor Hirohito a telegram, just today. Come on now, they would have to be idiots to attack the U.S." The captain chuckles once again.

169

"You will be the idiot! You will be! It will happen! You must prevent it! Tell them, Jackson! Tell them!"

Jackson just stands there and mouths the words. "It's over, honey."

"Kids! Tell them! Tell them they will all diiiiiiie!!!" She is roughly carried away while kicking and screaming. "No! Grandfather! Grandfather!"

"Wow, Captain! She thinks you're her grandfather now. She's certifiable, that one is." says the seaman.

The captain tells his crew to take Klara and Jackson away. He turns, faces us and says, "You ok?"

We all nod in the affirmative.

"Charles, how about you son?"

"Yeah, Dad, I'm fine."

"Daaaad???" Pete asks.

"Yeah," says Chuck, "US Coast Guard Captain Charles Bailey, Sr., my father."

"Well, how did you . . . How did you know?"

"I rang him at a phone booth when you guys were reviewing the map. I simply told him that some friends needed help and where we were headed."

"Good thinking, Chuck!" Pete says while slapping Chuck on the back.

"Yeah, man, just a few seconds more and, well, who knows what would have happened?" says Abby.

I think we all know what would have
170

happened. Klara was determined to do what she set out to do. Our next stop was to six Japanese carriers headed for Oahu. That could have easily meant the end of all of us, attack on Pearl Harbor or not.

"Well it's a pleasure to meet you, sir. Chuck, umm . . . I mean, Charles, Jr. has really helped us out a lot tonight." I praise.

"That's fine, that's just fine. Now let's head back towards Pearl."

"Pearl? Shouldn't we head, like, um . . . to the jail or something or . . ." I ask. Pearl is the last place I want to be.

"We are, boy, The United States Coast Guard goes hand in hand with the United States Navy, so that's where we're headed. The Coast Guard is right next door to Pearl. We'll get these matters all taken care of and then notify your folks of your whereabouts. They are probably worried sick. It's almost 3 a.m.!"

3 a.m. This wasn't over yet. Klara was right of course. Pearl Harbor was still going to be attacked. Even though the men mocked her and labeled her, "crazy." Everything was going to happen just as the history books have told us over the past 70 years. And now we are going to be there. Right there, at the heart of it. We are going to be at Pearl Harbor when it is being attacked by the Japanese.

CHAPTER SEVENTEEN

We set sail, around Oahu's western coastline with a heading directly for Pearl Harbor. Honestly, I would rather hunker down in the observation bunker on Diamond Head. Who knows where the safest air-attack hiding place would be? After all, we are on an island, a very easy target.

Abby, Pete and I share a blanket. Pete and Abby are shivering, more so because of the shock of it all rather than the actual temperature of the air, the water or the breezy ride. Their eyes are both shut but I am pretty sure they are still awake. I scoot over next to Chuck to talk to him.

"Chuck, since your dad did not believe Klara at all, I am guessing that you did not mention anything about the attack, right?"

"No, I didn't. Not yet anyways. Don't worry, Jon. I won't change this . . . this unfortunate historical event, but I *will* warn my father so there is ample time for him, no, for *us*, to escape or at least to seek shelter and to tell my mom and sis what to do."

"Ok, well, I hate to leave you with all of that to do but, well, we have got to get outta here. As interesting as it would be to see something of this

172

magnitude take place, I really don't want to and I know Abby and Pete don't wanna either."

"Yeah, that's understandable, Jon. You three have been through a lot. I'll help you get the time travel machine thingies as soon as we disembark."

"Thanks a million, Chuck. I really mean that, bud."

I reach out with my fist to pound his fist and quickly remember that in the 1940's, a fist aimed at someone is a definite sign of aggression. "Oh," I say, "Sorry!" I transform my fist into an open hand and extend my palm. Chuck does the same and we shake.

I will leave it at that. Who am I to tell him not to warn his own family? I mean, I would do it. And sadly, who's to say his father will actually believe him. I sure hope Charles Sr. does, for Chuck's sake.

We reach our destination. It's still dark out but, looking back at the horizon, I can see a faint hint of red. The sun will rise soon. Not only the giant ball of fire that we call the sun, but also the Japanese rising sun; the emblem on every flag that will be worn by the attacking Japanese pilots, and the meatball that adorns the panel of every striking plane.

I rise to my feet as the boat slows. The other vessel, carrying Klara and Jackson, pulls into port right alongside us. They exit their ship first. A seaman hops off and turns around to assist the handcuffed Klara followed by Jackson. Another shipmate shoves Jackson in the back with a baton. A

173

third guy bends over and picks up Jackson's hat as well as Klara's bag full of inventions. They exit their ship by walking down a long platform that ends at the dock.

"Hey, mister, can I have my toys back?" asks Abby, acting as if she is a lot younger, while she points to Klara's bag. The seaman pushes himself off the boat and onto the dock. He turns back at Abby, looks down at her, opens the bag and looks in it.

"Sir," he calls to his superior, standing a few yards up the dock. "Do I give this back to the girl?"

"Let me see," says the officer as he walks over to the bag, leaving Klara and Jackson with some other seamen. The officer retrieves the bag, opens it fully, reaches his hand inside and shuffles through the items. We all look intently. This was either the brightest or the dumbest thing Abby has ever done.

"These yours, young la . . ." he asks, looking up at Abby.

"Yes, sir!" Abby chimes in before letting him finish his question.

Klara turns around after Jackson clues her in on what was going on.

"What! Those are not toys! Those are my grandfather's inventions! Unhand them right now!"

The man restraining Klara tightens up a bit and tugs her back. She turns around and hisses at him like the snake that she is.

"Inventions! Ha ha," says the officer as he continues to rummage through the bag. "These are

174

just toys from the local toy store. See?" he says as he points to one of the inventions from the bag. "Some kinda Erector Set or, or a Tinker Toy or something I'd say. Here ya go, kids," he says handing it over. "Dizzy broad! Ha ha! Toys!"

"NOOOO!" Klara screams as the officer walks her and Jackson down the dock and towards the nearest building. She continues to scream and shuffle her feet as she tries to get lose. "Grandfather! Grandfather! I am so sorry!!!!" The door shuts behind her and peace and quiet resume.

Abby politely claims her reward and closes the top of the bag very nonchalantly, as if we didn't just obtain about twenty Nazi inventions under the guise of toys. Who would have thought it would be so easy? That was good thinking on Abby's part. She will never let us forget this one!

Chuck shakes his head and smiles in disbelief. "Captain," he says to his father as he steps off the ship, "When do you get off tonight?"

"Oh, not tonight, junior, don't get off 'till noon, Son." He offers his hand to Abby and she accepts as he helps her off board. Pete and I follow her lead.

"Captain, I need to talk to you."

"Junior, now you take your friends and wait over at that depot," his father says, pointing to a large brick building.

"But, Captain!"

"Do as your told, Son."

175

"Dad! I need to talk to you!"

His father is silent and looks up at Chuck taking note of the emotion in his voice.

"Yes, Son, what is it?"

"Please come home with us tonight. Don't stay here for your shift. Just tell them there is a family emergency or something. Please. Dad. I'm begging you."

"Junior, we just foiled a major terrorist plot. And we owe it all to you! Now I know things are shaky and your adrenaline is running, as is mine, but I gotta get these clowns processed. The paperwork alone will take me 'till morning."

"Please Dad, I just . . . I just have a really bad feeling about things," Chuck admits.

"Junior, take hold of yourself, Son. Now don't start believing any of her hogwash stories about the Japanese. Everyone is on alert. We have the brand new SCR-270 radar system up on Opana Point! If anything comes our way, we'll know it! Everything is fine, boy, just fine."

"Dad. Sir. Please. Just trust me. You trusted me with that call, right? Trust me again."

Chuck has a stern, serious look on his face. His father pauses at his son's sober expression and replies, "Son, I'll see what I can do. You know that my job is not one of the safest jobs around. But . . . if it means that much to you, well . . . I will do my best to get off early."

Chuck is happy, but still unsure. He smiles a

partial, insincere smile, thanks his father, shakes his hand as if they just met and turns back towards us.

Pete, not too empathetic, leans to my ear and says, "Dude, can we get outta here?"

"Yeah, I know, Pete. We have to leave Pearl."

"Well, yeah Jon, but I meant home. Ya know, *home* home. But yeah, I guess we better get outta here first, huh? This stuff is about to go down, right?"

"Yeah, man, and soon, too soon."

But we can't leave right yet. For one, the device is frozen again. It's still locked to our coordinates and date from yesterday. Besides that, a guard is approaching us. I don't think our time here is up after all.

"Hey guys, I just need a brief statement from you before you head out, alright? Just follow me over to central."

"Yes, sir," we say in unison.

We walk across the worn down grass that lies between the depot and the central office building and follow the guard inside. He opens a door to a small office right off the entrance. He tells us to stay seated in the lobby until he can gather the paperwork. Klara, Jackson and the others can be seen through a tiny window in a door at the end of a nearby hall. They are locked in one giant jail cell, all of them, even the hired help. Klara walks around in circles behind her cell bars.

177

"I need you guys one at a time. Ok . . . um . . . Charles, please step inside." the guard calls from the office.

Abby gets up from her seat and walks closer to where the prisoners are being held. I call for her to come back but she has a mind of her own. She walks down the hall and makes eye contact with Klara through the little window in the door. She opens the door and proceeds inside. At this point, I tap Pete's knee to tell him we need to follow her.

She opens the door as we catch up. She walks right up to Klara. Abby hasn't forgotten that she was tied up for quite a long time and it was all due to Klara's wild escapade.

"You know, I am really sorry that you never knew your grandfather and all. And I know that many people were forced to work for the Nazis, although I am not sure about your grandfather. But either way, you are a vile, terrible and utterly sad person! And I hope you stay locked up here, FOREVER!"

Her voice rises toward a shrieking scream, reminding us that she is, indeed female and has a couple octaves higher than us. Her scream alerts the sleeping guard in the corner as he quickly shoos us away, redirecting us to the front lobby.

Pete lags behind, peaks his head in the bars and says, "Hey, evil Nazi lady, how 'bout telling us how to fix that crappy device your grandfather made so we can get back to the twenty-first century!"

I rush back and pull Pete away just in time

178

for him to miss the giant loogi that Klara spits at him.

"Hey!" He yells towards her with a face of aggression. We head to the front and take our turns being interviewed by the guard.

Our stories are the same. We didn't have to concoct anything or make sure our stories jived; they simply did. We were all wise enough to know what could be said and what should and shouldn't be said. We simply told the interviewer that the strange man and woman captured us and forced us to drive them to their gunboats where the other men met us. We did, however tell them that she believed she was protecting us from attack, albeit for malicious reasons.

"Charles, go ahead and get those kids home, Ok? Do as your father told you," the guard says.

"Yes, sir," Chuck says as he heads to the door.

We head back to the Woody which is being driven to the front of the building by another guard. He puts it in park and exits.

"Thanks, Geeeeeeves," Pete says to the cop. The guard replies with a smirk and some words under his breath.

"Pete, he's a guard, not your own personal valet!" scolds Abby as she hops in the passenger seat. Pete watches in dismay since he was aiming for the shotgun seat himself. Even a trip back in time doesn't change Pete's brash sense of humor. The rest of us hop in the car. Chuck starts driving off even before I get a chance to slam my door shut.

We drive away from the Coast Guard, away from Pearl Harbor and away from Chuck's father. Chuck is trying his best to mask his emotions behind his body language and facial expression, but it just isn't working.

I can't blame him. Worrying about family is a tough thing. I remember Mom last year, worrying so much about her kid brother. He was shot down in the Middle East on a routine mission in some country that was housing a suspected terrorist cell. She thought we had lost him forever. He was reported as MIA.

Mom wasn't the same for those four days. She sat alone waiting by the phone for something, anything, regarding news on her brother. I mean, we were all upset and worried of course, and prayed, everything that would be expected. But, understandably, it was extremely difficult for her. He was finally found, severely beaten and dehydrated, but still alive, thank God. It took a while, but Mom was back to her normal, amazing self.

CHAPTER EIGHTEEN

It's about a quarter 'till seven now. "Tempest Fugit," I say to myself, after reading my watch. I think that's how you pronounce it. I've only had one year of Latin. But time really does fly, even when it's not, well, *your* time.

We are about 30 miles away from Pearl, once again, headed towards the North Shore, hoping that some of the boats are still there and aren't being guarded. It's very doubtful, but, if so, we can easily take one and get away from the island. Even if we can't take a boat it'll be safer in the North where there are less people and no major bombing targets. I still feel bad we can't warn the rest of the islanders.

Chuck pulls over at a little gas station to fill up the thirsty wagon. He gets out, leaves the door open and begins to pump.

This would be a good time to check the device. I wonder if it's working yet. We need it now more than ever. I dunno if it's out of power or if there is a short with that thermal switch thing or what.

"Pete, can you hand me the device?"

181

"Sure man. Where is it?" Pete asks.

"Should be in the bag in the back?" I reply.

"Houston," Pete says, followed with a static sound effect, "we have a problem."

"What do you mean, Pete?" I ask while turning around.

"Sorry, bud, but . . . there is no bag."

"What!!!?" I scream.

"Dude, I said there is no bag! I dunno where it is! I don't see it, do you?"

"What? That can't be!"

"Um, I dunno, Jon," Pete says as he frantically searches the back of Chuck's wagon. I look over at Abby, once again awakened by the commotion. She re-adjusts herself in her seat and bites her lower lip, looking like she needs to say something.

"What . . . is it . . . Abby?" I say, already knowing what her response will be. She takes a deep breath and looks down towards the floor and says, "I am so sorry, Jon. I must have left it back at the waiting room when I went to give Klara a piece of my mind. I was just so frustrated, for real! Oh, man. I fail. Sorry guys!"

"Fail? Fail? This is the epitome of an EPIC fail Abby! How could you forget something that's so important?"

"I am so sorry, Jon! How much time is there before the attack?"

"It doesn't matter. We have to go back now

182

or else we will be stuck here forever!" I scream as I see Chuck finish paying for the gas. We make eye contact through the shop window and I wave at him to hurry. He agrees with a thumbs up while taking the receipt in his other hand. He knows we have to hurry, but we have to hurry even more so now. We gotta get back to Pearl and leave again before the attack and we are running out of time.

"Hurry, Chuck! Hurry!" I yell as he exits the shop.

"Ok, ok, bud, we're gonna be fine, don't worry!" He says as he fake jogs back to the car.

"No, man! We have to go back, back to Pearl."

"Ha ha, go on, quit pulling my leg."

"No! Really, man. I know it sounds like a major death wish but honestly, the device is back there. The whole bag was left back there!"

"What? How the hell could we forget that? Who was holding it?"

"No time. Let's just go back. We gotta hurry! Let's go!"

"God help us!" says Chuck as he hops in the car and slams on the gas pedal.

It's 7:15 a.m. now. We might be able to get back right before the attack, if we don't encounter any obstacles that is. I think the initial attack was at 7:55. Or was it 7:45? Wow. You never think you need to know the exact details in history class. You just try to get the gist of things. Boy, how this info would have helped us now. Oh well.

Abby feels really bad. She should. It was her idea to ask for the bag and she was the one holding it. However, now is not the time to chastise her. We all have to stick together and fight for our safety, our lives. We are about to be in a warzone, literally.

She cries on Pete's lap while he consoles her as best as he can. He begins to sing the theme song of her favorite yellow spongy cartoon friend. She forces a laugh and shuts her eyes.

Chuck has the peddle floored. These old cars look awesome but they definitely do not handle well. With the speed we are going now we can feel every bump, pothole and crack we encounter. Also, having neither power steering nor breaking doesn't make me feel any safer. The only thing that makes me feel safe is, if we hit anything, we are pretty much in a tank. So, there are no worries there. Just, maybe taking a corner too hard, followed by a couple of acrobatic barrel roles, save the net; that could be a problem. We may die before the Japanese even have a chance to kill us!

Chuck continues to speed down the highway. We are halfway there, halfway back to the primary target of the Japanese. He checks his watch with every other blink. With any other free chance, he takes time to look at the sky behind us in his rearview mirror. He and I basically take turns doing so. No sign of any planes yet. If we can just keep this rate of speed up we'll be able to make it back in time. Well, we won't be able to leave the island or get that far away, but at least we'll be able to get out of the main target zones in time enough to hunker down.

Talk about a crazy time here in Hawaii: We had no sleep, we were chased, kidnapped and now we're driving dangerously fast in a time where airbags are only a dream. Not exactly my idea of a first visit to Hawaii.

We remain silent. What can we say? We are tired, hungry, thirsty, and we don't smell very good either. We have been perspiring so much, not just due to all of our physical activity and don't mind the fact that we haven't showered in a while, but the emotions, the anxiety and adrenaline flowing through all of us. Everything is taking its toll.

Abby, in the back seat, has dozed off on Pete's lap. Her somber dreams don't last long however as Chuck hits another pothole and sends us about a foot into the air. The springs in the wagon, as well as in the back bench, compress and then expand. Pete flies up and hits his head on the back headliner. The silence is broken.

"Sorry, Pete," says Chuck.

"No worries, man. You're doing fine, just keep going and get us there."

As we get closer to the southern shore we only encounter a bit more traffic. But even the traffic here is very light compared to last night. Thankfully, it's early on a Sunday morning. Some things don't change. Most people are still at home sleeping, attending Sunday service, eating breakfast or just relaxing.

We approach the base. I tell Chuck to slow down or else the guards will never let us get close. He heeds my warning and lifts his foot off the gas. Some men jog in formation, while a few others prepare to raise the American flag outside the Coast Guard's main office. I am sure the same is happening, not too far away, at Pearl. I am anticipating hearing the familiar trumpet wake up call, *Reveille*, but I think it's still a bit too early.

Chuck slams on his brakes when entering a parking space in front of the building. We slide on some gravel and end up hitting a wooden post that identifies the office. My door is already opened with my right foot on the ground before we come to a complete stop. I sprint over to the building where we were interviewed. I pull the doorknob as hard as I can to thrust the door open, but it won't budge. It's locked! I try again and again but it just won't give. Not again! I turn around and face the guys in the Woody. They look as hopeless as I feel right now.

I feel a hand on my shoulder and instinctively throw back my fist like a bad Kung Fu movie from the seventies. I'm as jumpy as can be. I almost forgot that Jackson and Klara were locked up safe and sound. I turn around to see the guard who interviewed us earlier.

"Hey, kid, watch it! That coulda hurt!" he says as he rubs his nose, the only part I made contact with, "I just ran to get a cup a joe. Whatdaya need?"

"Oh, sorry, sir, just a little on edge."

"I'll say. You stay away from my coffee then! Ok?" He laughs.

"Yeah, well, we kinda left something here, sir. And I was just trying to get it."

"Oh, yeah," he says as he shoves his newspaper under his right armpit, sticks the key in the door and watches his coffee teeter back and forth in his other hand. "The bag of toys, right?"

"Yes! Yes, sir, that's it! Did you find it?"

"Yeah, kid. It fell behind the row of chairs, see?"

He pushes the door open but loses his coffee all over the doorway as well as his hand. He lets out a giant yell.

"Are you ok?" I ask as I force myself through the door, searching for the bag.

"Yeah, kid, thanks. As if you care." He says under his breath.

It's true. I was rude, but we are about to be attacked. I don't have time to offer him help with his hand. But . . . I can offer him some other advice. I can warn him, somehow.

I spot the bag, grab it and head back towards the door. He stands there, wiping his hand and legs with his newspaper. I can hear Klara in the back room. She is screaming for someone to let her out. "You will be sorry!!! The attack is imminent!!" she cries.

187

"Don't you have your own laundry room downstairs, sir? I, um, thought I saw a sign earlier."

"Yeah, yeah we do, kid. Thanks."

"I think you should get down there as fast as you can, ya know, to save your clothes from being stained, I mean."

"Yeah, I guess you're right. My superiors wouldn't let me live this one down. Besides, those jokers in the back aren't going anywhere anytime soon."

"That is true, sir. And uh, ya know . . . maybe you could just stay down in the basement and read your paper while your clothes are drying."

"Yeah, kid, sure."

I know it sounds strange but what else could I do? I am doing my best to help him, to help whoever I can. My old ideals of preventing change in the past have already fallen by the wayside. Might as well save a life.

CHAPTER NINETEEN

I rush back to the wagon, throw the bag to Peter and yell, "Drive! Drive!"Chuck floors it, once again. The tires squeal, slip on the gravel, finally gain traction and we set off. I am not sure where, but anywhere is better than here.

Pete takes out the primary temporal device, the one that we need, and carefully examines it. It's still dead. It's blank. But at least it's in our possession again.

He switches the thermal switch back and forth, on and off, over and over again to no avail. Even though the secondary tracking device is right next to it, the primary device's green light is no longer lit. Pete shoves it back into the bag and holds it tightly on his lap as we continue to drive out of the base.

But we're too late. There is something on the horizon in the distance. It could only be one thing: Japanese Zeros. Chuck slams on the breaks in awe and terror as we all poke our heads out of the

189

windows and gaze at the oncoming onslaught. The little dots get larger and larger and come in greater numbers.

They say your life flashes before your eyes when you fear you are about to meet your demise. Now I know that's true: Mom and Dad at my first little league game, trying to sneak a peek at Santa but falling asleep under the Christmas tree, learning how to ride my bike. All of those memories flash, like a movie, in my mind.

"You were right!" Chuck shouts. "My God, you guys were right! I mean, I believed you, but, I just, I just didn't want it to happen!"

"I know, Chuck. It's ok, just drive. Drive!!!!" I say, snapping out of my mental movie.Chuck also regains himself and floors it once again.

The bombers and fighters, the notorious Zeros, continue to press south, coming closer and closer to us. The loud whine from their engines maintain, growing louder, stronger and faster. Yet, no one else seems to notice them. The locals must be a little too used to hearing low flying aircraft near the bases.

Chuck is driving wildly now, running up curbs and knocking over several metal trashcans. He frantically peers through the front windshield, watching the planes approach.

"ERRRRRRRRRRRRRRR!" The wagon's brakes squeal as our front right fender slams into the left rear quarter panel of a taxi cab. Our force pushes the taxi to do a one-eighty. It is now parallel to us but facing the other direction. Chuck overcorrects the steering and slams us into a light pole.

These machines are tanks, alright. There is some damage, but nothing compared to what a modern accident would have looked like. The wagon is smoking now, however, and Chuck can't get it started.

After checking to see if everyone is alright, we slide out of the seats and exit the car via the right passenger doors. The doors on the left, including the driver's side door are blocked by the taxi.

The driver curses at us through his window but then recants upon noticing that we are, as he puts it, "just kids." Chuck points up to the sky. The planes are upon us now. He points them out to the cabi. The driver, still in his taxi, turns his head over his left shoulder in confusion. His eyes grow wide in fear as he realizes this car accident is just the start of his bad day.

"Run, guys! Run," I yell. "Take cover!" The four of us run over to the nearest visible building, praying that it has a basement. We're still on Coast Guard property but are not sure what the building is, as it bears no markings. It doesn't matter. Chances are it will soon be destroyed. I just hope there is not an adjoining ammo depot of some sort.

Everything is in slow motion as we run. The Pacific is right behind us and Pearl Harbor itself is only about 500 yards away.

191

The planes are right above us now, like a swarm of bees. They are no longer a secret. Everyone sees and hears them. They are as inconspicuous as a pumpkin in a Christmas tree lot.

We are only about twenty feet away from the wagon when it hits me. I can't believe we left the bag . . . again. I run back to the wagon with all my might. The cabi has now exited his car and is still standing there in dread, gazing up at the impending doom.

I throw myself inside the Woody's open rear door. Thankfully the bag is in plain sight this time; no need to hunt for it. I rip it out from under the seat and head back towards the others.

As I run to catch up with them I hear the commotion of a lady screaming and people panicking and running, responding to the sounds of the first explosions in the harbor. The explosions almost sound like the Fourth of July. In lieu of the accompaniment of joyfully colored fireworks, however, are deadly fires.

We are less than a minute into it and people are frantically scurrying everywhere like party goers at an under aged party when the cops show up. I almost catch up to Pete and the others when I hear the strafing of a Japanese fighter. I look back while continuing to run and see Chuck's wagon get shot to pieces. It gets hit in the radiator and a huge burst of steam comes blowing out from under the hood.

We continue to run to the nearest building, and hear the sound of more bombs and torpedoes hitting their targets. The air raid siren is now sounding at full alarm. America is under attack. We will enter the war tomorrow and I am here to witness it all, first hand.

I'd rather be at home, up in the oak, reading a comic book, hanging with Pete or even doing my summer assignment. Anything would be better than this. Learning about history and actually *living* it are two different things. I guess we take things too lightly in our day and age. We sit back and watch a film or TV series about World War II or joke around and act it out in a video game. But when the movie is over, I am safe and all the actors get a hefty paycheck to *pretend* they were fighting. If my character dies in a game, I just have to hit restart from the last checkpoint. This is all too real for me.

Just as we reach the building, I hear the familiar whining of a plane engine. It's familiar only because of those WWII movies. But hearing it in real life is ten times different. Even the video games, with their digital surround sound, don't give it justice. It's getting louder and louder, closer and closer, faster and faster. It slams into the roof of the building adjacent to our destination. At impact the propeller slices through the roof tiles. One of the propeller blades flies off and spins through the air. It ends up being lodged into the side of a mighty palm tree as if deposited by a tornado.

Chuck throws Abby and Pete to the ground and uses his body to shield them. I fend for myself.

193

My hands instinctively come up to my face to protect my eyes from dirt, glass and other debris. My right leg however is not so lucky. A piece of glass cuts me from my knee to my shin. It doesn't feel that deep though and thankfully doesn't impede my movement as I crawl across the ground searching for more coverage.

Klara's bag was thrown from my shoulder when I took my initial dive for safety. With the top of the bag partially open, I see the lights of the primary device! It's back on! I don't know how or why, but it's back on! Something must have jarred the thermal switch and it corrected itself to its default position. Maybe it was the vibrations of the plane crashing into the building or the car accident with the taxi. I really don't care. Either way, it's on and that's all we need.

I reach into the bag and pull out the device. I want to shout over towards the others but it's too much of a challenge to be heard over the gunfire and explosions. Flaming debris from the neighboring building is still showering from above. The bulk of the first raid of fighters and bombers has made its way over us. They are now sending their death blows over the harbor.

I wave my arms at the others and scream, trying to get their attention while holding the device in the air. All three of them are hunched over, attempting to find cover wherever they can. I should follow their lead.

Chuck finally looks up and catches a glimpse

of me waving my arms as fast as a Zero's propeller. He reaches over and grabs Pete on the shoulder with one hand while pointing towards me with the other.

"Look! It's on! The device is on!" I faintly make out Chuck scream towards Abby and Pete. They gather together and, still crouched over, attempt to get closer to me. I do the same. We finally meet up at a large chunk of wreckage from the downed plane.

"It's on! We can go home!" I shout over the noise of the attack.

"Hurry up and push it, Jon," demands Pete.

I turn the device around and focus intently on the keypad but am interrupted by a huge explosion. We flinch as the earth trembles around us. I look back at the harbor and see fire and smoke reaching high into the early morning sky. Whoever had that ship as their target hit the bull's eye, that's for sure. Something *that* huge could only have been the U.S.S. Arizona, the strike that claimed the most lives at Pearl Harbor. I am motionless and speechless as I watch the Pacific Fleet fall to this horrendous attack. I start to say a quick Hail Mary for all the lives being lost but Abby cuts me short.

"Jon, hurry! We gotta go!"

She grabs the device from my hand and begins to finger the keypad. The gunfire and explosions die down as many of the planes head to the North, flying over us on their way back to their carriers. Round one must be over.

"What is today's date? Like, our today's

195

date?" Abby questions. Pete responds with, "August twentieth." Abby punches in the date and then looks down at the coordinate screen.

"No, way! I don't know what to put here! We could end up in the Pacific Ocean in the middle of nowhere, Jon! We need a map or something!"

There is no time for running around and looking for a map now. But we do need the latitude and longitude coordinates. That's a given.

"Hey!" Pete says, "I can help!"

"Yeah, sure you can, Pete. How in the world could you help?" Abby scolds.

"What's that supposed to mean, huh?" Pete looks genuinely offended.

"I did a science fair project a few years back where I had to measure some different coordinates and then put them into this equation thing that my partner made. Well, I dunno what we did actually. She did all the work, but I did one thing! I rode my scooter all over town with my dad's handheld GPS and jotted down the coordinates. I looked at those things so many times that I ended up memorizing all of them! Well, ok, my partner, she made me memorize them. I had to give the presentation all alone on account of her coming down with the . . ."

"Ok, fella, we get it. We get it. You guys gotta get outta here now," says Chuck. "What are some coordinates?"

"Well, I can give ya the ones for the treehouse, Jon!"

"No, No Pete. Remember what happens? The more people who travel, the more chance there is of losing the device in the process. It has to be some place open, like a field or something."

"The park in the center of town! I know that one, Jonny! Woohoo! I know that one!"

Pete leans over and punches a series of numbers into the device: the numbers that Pete remembers from a failed science fair project from the fifth grade. But it's the best shot we got.

The red numbers pop up immediately under the keypad on the screen. We are ready to go.

"Wait! There is no place on this thing for an exact time, just a day," notices Abby.

"So? Who cares what time it is? Let's just go!" replies Pete.

"Yeah but what if we see ourselves or something, we just . . ."

"It doesn't matter, we have to go before the bombing begins again or we won't be seeing anything, Abby!" I exclaim.

"Ok, Ok!"

I reclaim the device and slide the cover off of the trigger.

"Wait!" Chuck says as he holds out his hand like a stop signal. He runs over to an orange and white wind sock that lies on the ground. It is still attached to its toppled poll. Chuck rips off a piece of the orange material and runs it over to us.

"Tie this around it. It'll help you find it if it

gets separated from you again."

"Chuck, that's a great idea! Thanks, man!" I say while patting him on the back.

"Ok, guys, is everyone ready?"

"Did you really have to ask that, Jon?" asks Abby. I suppose she's right. We are nothing but ready to get back home.

I approach Chuck and say, "Thanks for all of your help. We could not have survived without you! I really wish there was some way for us to keep in touch, but I don't think I can send you and email back in time!"

"Ha ha, he-mail? Like when a guy writes a letter to another guy?" Chuck asks.

"No, no. Nevermind. Anyways thanks a million, bud. Go find your father and take care of yourself. You guys will survive this! America will survive this and many more trials in the future. You just gotta hold on and have faith, ok, bud?"

"Ok, Jon, you do the same. Safeguard the future for us, for *all* of us!" Chuck says as he waves goodbye while he is backing up to maintain a safe distance from us. We wave back.

"Ready, guys? Ok, everyone hold on to each other. Pete, how confident are you about these numbers?"

"They're good, Jon! Trust me!"

"Ok, then, here we go!"

CHAPTER TWENTY

A loud crash, bang and sense of heat come over us, right as I pull the trigger. For a minute, I am not sure if the device was working or if we were just hit by another attacking plane. No, it's working. The familiar bright light and accompanying temperature fluxuation have returned. It feels as if I'm falling through space in an endless tunnel of light, wind and noise.

We continue to hold onto each other. I am able to see Abby and Pete but am unable to say anything at all. And then, just as sudden as it all started, it is over. Thankfully, Pete was right on this one. We end up in the park, just as he had said. It's apparently around the time we left because the storm is at about the same intensity now as it was then.

The thunder cracks and howls as we are shaken out of our time travel stupor. The drops of heavy rain sting my face as I look around. We get up and check to see if we are ok. Pete and I both pay close attention to Abby to make sure she is alright. After this entire event, being kidnapped and all, she doesn't like the added attention. She shrugs her shoulder and shoos us both away, insisting that she is fine.

"I got it! I got it!" she claims, as we help her up and she pats herself clean.

"Good call on the coordinates, Petey," she says as she looks around at the wide open park.

"Thanks, Abby. Now, we just have to find the time stick!"

"Ha ha, *time stick*? I kinda like that, Pete!" she says.

We spread out, looking for the device in the pouring rain. It takes about ten minutes before I realize we still have the bag of Klara's other devices, including the secondary device. All we have to do is use that one to locate the primary, the same way that Klara and Jackson tracked us down in Hawaii.

"You guys, come here!" I yell. Pete and Abby come jogging back.

"Did you find it?"

"No, but look," I say, reaching into the bag. "Remember? All we have to do is use this!"

"Good thinking, bro!" Pete says. "But one question: why didn't they use this secondary one to locate the primary one in the first place? They would have saved all that time and trouble searching around the neighborhood."

"I dunno. You know she said it still has some bugs in it. I am just hoping it works for us."

I dig through the bag of "toys" and find the

secondary device. Thankfully it's already turned on and honing in on the primary. It is illuminated with a solid pattern of lights. This means the most important one, the main device, is nearby.

We walk around the wide open field in the park, using the secondary device like a metal detector, swaying back and forth, back and forth.

Sure enough, there it is. It rests against the trunk of a tree, slightly obstructed by a picnic table. Its solid green light is a shining beacon in the gloomy darkness of the storm. Chuck's orange fabric is still tied to it. I sure hope he is doing alright.

We can rest now. The device is safe. We are safe. And Jackson and Klara are tucked away in a 1941 prison.

"Holy . . . "

"What is it, Pete?"

"Look!"

I look in the direction of Pete's extended index finger, pointing across the park. Of course . . . it's the white van. In the driver seat is none other than our favorite public enemy number two, Jackson!

"Dude! How can that be? They were locked up! We just left them! We have the only devices."

Pete was right. This was crazy.

"I dunno, Pete. Come on. But stay low!"

We slowly and stealthily head towards the van which is now barreling down the road.

A crash of lighting smacks behind us and makes Pete surpass Abby and me, putting him in the lead, although still at a snail's pace. We have lost the van for now, but we cut across to the other end of the park and head in the same direction.

"Come on, guys! He's headed towards the plantation house!" Pete says. The plantation house. The same plantation house where Pete mowed over the device. The same plantation house where we sought refuge from Jackson's henchmen by hiding in the bushes. And the very same plantation house where Abby was kidnapped.

"Jon! Jon . . . I . . . I think I know when this is, I mean, I think . . . ," says Abby, stuttering and puzzled.

"Yeah, I know, Abb! I know exactly what you mean. But we just gotta make sure. Make sure . . . they are not back."

We keep running through the rain, splashing through puddles and dodging every lightning strike that seems to be right on our steps.

"Abby, what are you talkin' about? Jon what is it? What is it, man?" Pete shouts while turning his head over his shoulder, continuing to lead the way. He stops, suddenly, as if running into an invisible tree. I stop quick enough to avoid running into him but the slippery sidewalk has other plans and I knock him to the ground.

"Sorry, dude." I say. "Why did you stop all of the sudden?" Pete gets up as if nothing happened. His eyes are still fixed in front of him. I look up but don't see anything. I scoot closer to him and try to look from his exact vantage point. It works.

Through the bushes, the brush and the pouring rain, there we were. I mean, really. There *we* were, the earlier versions of us, hiding from Jackson's henchmen.

"We gotta save us! Abby! Abby!" cries Abby as she tries to get closer. Pete and I both grab her, holding her back by her shirttail.

"Stop it! Guys, let me go! We gotta warn them. I mean us . . . I mean them!"

"No, Abby! Come on, didn't you learn anything?" I insist as I pat her on her back. "Everything will be fine. We know how this turns out. Everything is gonna be ok!" It's hard to tell in the pouring down rain but I'm pretty sure she is starting to tear up.

"It's not ok! You weren't kidnapped and tied and taped up and slapped and spit on!"
She begins to cry. Pete approaches her and gives her a hug. She falls limp into his arms. I motion for us to hide behind a pickup truck that is parked perpendicular to the plantation house.

We hop in the truck bed and easily maintain our view of the action via the truck's rear window. Abby screams in the distance. I look up and see Jackson grab her shoulder from behind. In the meantime, Pete holds Abby even tighter, shielding her eyes and ears from the events that have already transpired.

I tell her, "It has to happen like this, Abby!
203

It's in the past, what happened to us, even though it's going on right here, it happened to us in the past. We know how it all ends up. Look at us. We are all fine! I know it's painful, for all of us, and I can only imagine how scared you must have been. But we can't interfere. We just can't!"

"How is Jackson even here, Jon?" Pete asks? "He's still locked up right, with Klara I mean? And hopefully even injured in the attack on Pearl? I just don't get it? And how in the world can two of each of us exist at the same time? Is that even possible?"

"I don't know, Jon." Normally, I would play the older, smarter role. But I am not even going to pretend to come up with an answer. "I just don't know, guys. I mean . . . who knows the rules about time travel? It's a whole new world," I say while turning back and forth, watching the past us, as well as the current us.

"Abby, I think this is one part you'll want to see." Pete proclaims. Abby, emotionally and physically drained, musters up enough strength to gaze through the rear window of the truck. She is just in time to watch herself give Jackson that massive blow to the knee.

"Wow! That was a good one, wasn't it, guys. I sure let him have it!" Abby cracks a small smile between her teary eyes. Perhaps the reliving of kicking Jackson will calm her a bit. "So what do we do now, guys?" she asks.

What do we do now? Good question. This is

getting crazy. I mean, going back to witness the attack on Pearl Harbor was one thing, but spying on ourselves through the back window of a rusty old pickup definitely takes the cake.

"Here it comes, guys! Here it comes!" Pete says while kneeling at a full position and peaking over the top of the truck.

"Here *what* comes?" Abby asks.

"My big scene!" Pete exclaims as if he was the star of a movie. "I'm about to pull the trigger. Get ready, guys! Watch this!"

And there it is. Just as before and just like a few minutes ago, the moment we traveled through time. Only this time Pete and I get to see what it looks like from the other side.

A loud crack of thunder spanks the park with a huge flash of light, followed by a deep brassy rumble from the belly of the Earth. A giant wave of wind comes rushing upon us. Our assailants, including Jackson, are blown to their feet.

"Whoa!" says Pete, "that was totally epic!"

The henchmen get on their feet and continue to stare at our point of departure.
Jackson is still on the ground. It's quiet now and still. The storm has almost immediately subsided, the wind stopped and the rain has changed over to a spottier, sporadic drizzle.

"Get me up!" Jackson yells at the top of his lungs. The stubby man looks back but is still mesmerized. He does a double take, wipes his eyes clean and turns around. He takes his familiar roly poly strut back over to Jackson, and extends his hand to help him up. Jackson stands to his feet, although still heavily favoring the right leg. "Get the girl!" he yells. He points over towards the earlier Abby who is still standing at the gate. Her mouth and eyes are both wide open like those of a Jack o' Lantern on Halloween. Astonished by what just happened and also in disbelief that my, so called, "comic fantasy" was actually reality, we learn that Abby just stood there, frozen like a snowman. I can't really say I blame her. She just witnessed her two closest friends disappear.

I lean over the spare tire in the back of the truck and say, "So, *who* reads too many comic books now, huh, Abb?" She smirks and gives me a friendly push back towards the other side of the truck bed.

We hear a commotion and look back over towards the Abby in the plantation yard. Jackson and his crew head towards her. She turns and backs away from them in an effort to run but doesn't see another guy creeping behind her. He snatches her up. Kicking and screaming, she yells, "What did you do to them! What did you do to my friends! Where are they!?" Another guy drives up with the would-be ice cream van. The side door slides open and they throw Abby in the back, like a rag doll.

"Those bastards!" Pete says.

"Tell me about it," she says, "I still have this huge knot on my head from banging up against the side of the van."

"Sorry, Abby," says Pete, offering another consoling hug.

"Well, at least we know they got what they deserved," I say, "locked up in the past, that is."

"Yeah! Well, nobody said I wanted them dead," Abby says while frowning at the ground.

"Oh, believe me I am sure they are safe," I promise her. "They are incarcerated, but safe. That's for sure. No Japanese pilot would waste their bullets or bombs on an American prison. Besides, we wouldn't be that lucky." We smile and laugh as the van speeds off.

"I guess that's that," says Pete. "We can get back to our normal, boring lives again." He hops out of the back of the truck and lands on the wet pavement below.

"Not just yet," I say. "We can't be seen by Jackson or Klara or any of their crew. We have to lay low for a while, or at least for the night. Abby and I both jump out of the truck and shake off the rainwater as best as we can.

"That's a smart idea, Jon," Abby agrees. "It would be safer that way. We didn't leave right after they took me. Jackson and Klara argued a bit first. And after all of that, I don't wanna mess everything up."

"Then off to the oak it is, dudes!" Pete says, speaking in a stereotypical California surfer voice.

We head back to my house, back to the

treehouse and back to the happiness of normalcy. Although, I am pretty sure things will never be normal again for any of us.

Pete begins to hum and then eventually starts singing a Hawaiian song. He must have heard it on his trip there last year, because it does not ring a bell at all. "What's that?" I ask.

"Oh, this? It's the theme song from our trip! I just made it up. Like it?" Pete laughs as I smile and give his shoulder a soft punch. Abby just shakes her head.

CHAPTER TWENTY-ONE

By the time we reach the oak, the sun is shining bright and heavy through the breaking clouds. The steam that follows every summer storm rises from the pavement. We take a short cut through a vacationing neighbor's yard and hop over my back fence. We each take our turns climbing up the rope ladder. There really is no place like home.

I am the first one to make it inside the treehouse. As Pete finishes climbing up the ladder, he takes Klara's bag off his shoulder and pushes it up through the entrance. I grab it and place it aside, making sure Pete and Abby both make it up the slippery ladder without fail. Abby makes her way up but is halted by Pete. He turns around and says, "Sorry, no girls allowed!" At this point in time, Abby is in no joking mood at all. Pete extends his hand and quickly says, "JK! JK!" Some things will never change.

We each take a load off, letting gravity crash us down onto the bean bags. Pete and Abby share the duct-taped one. I was quick enough to get the good one. The place is still a terrible mess, but it is great to have some familiar surroundings again.

"So, what are we gonna do all night if we can't leave?" Pete asks.

"Good question," I reply. "Hand me the bag." Pete reaches over towards the entrance, picks up the bag and chucks it towards me as if it were full of marshmallows. Doesn't he remember that it is filled with one-of-a-kind Nazi inventions?

"Watch it, man! This stuff is irreplaceable!" Pete cringes and scrunches his mouth and neck to show he realizes that, once again, he is at fault.

I reach in the bag and say, "Ok, now let's see what we got here. Just remember! Don't push any buttons! No more adventures for today." I say as I give a semi-serious smile. Pete nods and Abby gives me a thumbs up.

I pull the first item out and lay it on the wooden floor. It's the secondary device, so nothing new there. At least we know Klara and Jackson won't be on our tails this time, not without this. I reach in the bag and pull out a second item. It's metal, deep purple in color and of a triangular shape. It reminds me of an old metronome my sixth grade band director had. He never used it though. It was more like a glorified paper weight. This item has the usual buttons and dials and displays, but as I said, there is no way I am messing with it now. I set it next to the other.

I reach into the bag once again. This time,

my hand comes back with a solid black sphere, about the size of a small grapefruit or maybe, a large orange. It feels as if it doesn't weigh a thing. It's got a glossy sheen but unlike the others, I see no apparent dials or switches or anything of that nature. It's nothing like the original two devices. Speaking of the two devices, I better make sure that the other one is still here.

I dig deep in the bag and shuffle through about fifteen other little metal trinkets. I shove my hand down to the bottom and finally feel it, the primary device. Bringing it up, I am careful not to trigger it.

It gets snagged on something as I pull it out of the bag. I yank a little bit and the device gets freed. I set it aside, being careful not to trigger it. I notice the display has turned off, once more.

"It was stuck on something," I explain.

"Another one of Wexler's inventions?" asks Abby.

"Probably, but it felt different," I say while reaching back to the bottom of the bag.

"Here," says Pete as he reaches for the bag and begins to empty it on the floor. A pile of odd items comes crashing out of the bag, accompanied by a book: a blueprint book.

"Look! There it is!" Pete shouts, "Klara was talking about this book! Who knew she had put it in the bag with the inventions!?" Pete and Abby nestle closer and surround me to get a better view as I start

211

thumbing through the book.

It reveals many of the schematics and layouts of the inventions we have already seen: the primary temporal device, the secondary one as well as the weird cloaking thing Klara used to conceal the boats. The newly discovered solid black sphere is also mentioned, opposite the page of the cloaking device. I pause on the black sphere page to determine its function.

"What's it say?" asks Pete.

"I dunno, man. I took Spanish, not German."

"Sucks to suck!" Pete says. This is something we'll have to get deciphered.

Abby, bored and frustrated from not knowing what the words say or mean, reaches over my lap and flips to the next page. But instead of turning directly to the next page, the flimsy book flops to the back, revealing a lot less pages than expected. She grabs the last page and flips it back and forth as if expecting to find the missing pages. But they aren't there, not at all. A huge chunk of the middle of the book has been torn out.

"Where's the rest of the book?" asks Pete.

"I dunno," I reply, "Looks like someone ripped them out." Someone ripped them out alright and in quite a hastily manner. Some of the last pages that were torn out still have segments of the bottom left corner attached in the book. There is a little bit of information on them, but, I guess not enough to be needed? Who took the pages? And when did they take them? And why?"

"Did Chuck rip them out?"

"No, Abby, don't be dumb. Why would Chuck do that? He's a cool guy." I proclaim.

"I dunno? I mean, I can't think of anyone else who had the opportunity to take them," she says as she slams the book shut.

"Well, Abb, we don't even know *when* they were taken. I mean, we didn't even realize we had this thing in the first place. Anyone could have ripped the pages out."

"What about the guard at the jail when you left it there?" Pete adds.

"Hey, that's not on me, or at least, not *just* me," Abby interjects. "It's on all of us. Besides, if it wasn't for me saying it was my bag of toys, we wouldn't have any of this."

"She's right again, Jon! Ha ha! "says Pete. We sit back and laugh as Abby gives Pete a friendly nudge. There is nothing we can do about it now. There's no way for us to know who took the pages or if they were taken before or after we took possession of the bag. Whoever took them obviously needed them fast. Why else would it just be a handful of pages? Why not the whole the book, or better yet, the whole bag of devices? I guess it is one of those things we will never know.

"Hey, kids! Kids! You up there?" Dad's voice travels up to the treehouse. "Pizza is here! Come on down!" I peak out door three. Sure enough, the pizza man jumps back into his little, pizza-sign-topped hatchback and takes off.

"I get the breadsticks!" yells Pete as he opens the main hatch and starts to descend the ladder. "No way, Pete! You hogged them last time!" Abby screams as she chases him down the tree.

I place the blueprint book on the highest shelf in the tree house, careful not to lose it in the mess on the floor, and put my history book on top of it. I shove the items back into the bag, place it in the back left corner of the tree house and follow Abby and Pete's lead. This adventure is over. The next one begins: the fight for the cherished bread sticks!